THEY CAME TO LEADVILLE

Griff Connors—A rawhide-tough stagecoach driver framed for robbery and murder. With the law on his tail, he must find the killers soon or forever ride the owlhoot trail.

Nan Harper—Unattractive in her own eyes, she gets plenty of attention from others who can see what she doesn't. Trying to save her stage line, she desperately need's Griff's help, yet she'd lose everything rather than risk his life.

Mike Malloy—The charismatic Irish mine worker— he is a man of peace who may have to fight to the death for his beliefs. All the others have run or died. He is determined to stand his ground against overwhelming odds.

Morgan Slaughter—Ruthless and cunning, he will allow nothing to stand between him and what he wants—be it a mine or a woman. And if he doesn't do the killing himself, there are others who will.

The Stagecoach Series
Ask your bookseller for the books you have missed

STAGECOACH STATION 20:
LEADVILLE

Hank Mitchum

Created by the producers of
Wagons West, White Indian,
and Saga of the Southwest.

Chairman of the Board: Lyle Kenyon Engel

BANTAM BOOKS
TORONTO • NEW YORK • LONDON • SYDNEY • AUCKLAND

STAGECOACH STATION 20: LEADVILLE

*A Bantam Book / published by arrangement with
Book Creations, Inc.*

Bantam edition/October 1985

Produced by Book Creations, Inc.
Chairman of the Board: Lyle Kenyon Engel

ISBN 0-553-25083-3

Published simultaneously in the United States and Canada

PRINTED IN THE UNITED STATES OF AMERICA

H   0 9 8 7 6 5 4 3 2 1

STAGECOACH STATION 20:

LEADVILLE

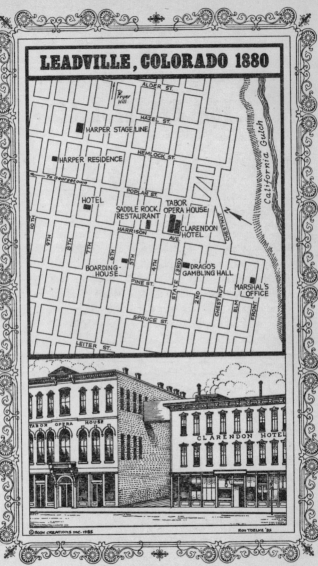

May, 1880

Griff Connors had no idea that trouble was coming. If there were any clues to be read, he somehow missed them—despite his ten years and more as a stagecoach driver across a wide sweep of the West. For all he could see, today was a run like any other run from Miles City to Billings, Montana, with no hint of anything wrong. All was going just as usual; and now, just as usual, he pulled out of the looping ribbon of stage road and into a meadow pocket. Ringed by tall pines, the rest stop had deep grass and a brisk mountain stream, where it was his custom to water the teams and rest them before taking the remainder of the haul.

His animals came to a stand of their own accord. He kicked on the brake and called down to his passengers, "We'll be stopping here about ten minutes. Chance for you all to stretch your legs."

But after that he glanced at the shotgun guard beside him on the high forward boot of the stagecoach, and something made him frown.

Lew Burke was a secretive sort; Griff could hardly claim to know him well, even after a winter of riding together. It wasn't odd that the man had said very little

1

during today's run, but now Griff saw the look on his narrow features, and he wondered.

Though it wasn't unnaturally warm for a May day in these Montana hills, he could see there was a faint sheen of sweat on the man's forehead and a tightening of his cheek muscles. Griff exclaimed, "You all right, Lew? Anything bothering you?"

The guard shot him a look. "No," Burke said shortly. But when Griff continued to study him, obviously not convinced, he shrugged and jerked a thumb toward the strongbox, below them in the boot of the stage. "I guess I can't forget there's a hell of a lot of money under our feet!"

That was a fact. Griff knew well enough what that box contained—a small fortune, by any man's reckoning, in greenbacks and coins destined for a new bank that was about to open its doors in a cattle town farther up the line. He said to Burke, "If anyone had wind of this shipment, I suppose there could be something to worry about, all right. But we've never yet had any trouble on this route, and there's been no leaks that I know of—no way that anybody could guess there's anything special about this run. So take it easy."

In reply, Lew Burke only shrugged again as he leaned to stow his shotgun under the seat. Griff left him there, with whatever was eating at him, and climbed down to see to his horses.

The coach door was already open. The three passengers—a ranchman, a storekeeper, and a man who had the earmarks of a traveling salesman—got stiffly out and with one accord wandered over to the creek bank, where they stood talking idly and looking at the water. Before unhitching his teams and leading them to the stream for a drink, Griff wanted to have a look at one of the lead horses, which was acting as though it might be about to throw a shoe. He was down on one knee, examining the hoof, when riders quietly came easing out of the timber, where they had been waiting.

He wasn't aware of them until it was too late. There

were three horsemen, masks covering their faces and weapons ready. As though by prearrangement they separated. The first that Griff knew of them was when he heard the thud of a hoof nearby and looked up into the sunlight at the silhouette of the mounted figure looming over him and the muzzle of a six-shooter pointed at his head.

Stunned, he seemed unable to move for an instant. Then he dropped the hoof and surged to his feet. Though a stage driver was not under any orders to carry a revolver, Griff had one in a belt holster around his waist. Before he could touch the weapon, the bandit told him gruffly, "Don't even think about it! Just ease that thing out of the leather and toss it in the crick."

Griff, a tall, soberly frowning man with sun-darkened face, brown eyes, and black mustache, stood a moment staring at the horseman. A cloth hood covered most of the bandit's face, though enough of a lantern jaw showed beneath its lower edge to reveal that he wore a patchy, poorly trimmed, reddish-colored beard.

The bandit gestured with the six-shooter in his fist. "That gun. Get rid of it—now!"

There was no real option. Griff took the revolver from its holster and reluctantly gave it a sideward toss into the rippled water of the nearby stream. Afterward he raised his hands shoulder high.

He saw now that another masked rider had the trio of passengers under control, standing with arms raised before his menacing six-gun. That left the third bandit, who walked his horse directly toward the coach. Still in his place atop the stage, the first hint Lew Burke seemed to have of what was afoot came in a warning that made him freeze, then slowly turn his head. If Burke had had a premonition earlier, it did him no good now. Without a word he obediently emptied his holster, dropping his six-shooter into the early spring grass beside the big front wheel. The shotgun quickly followed it.

The outlaw barked another order, and Griff Connors watched helplessly as the stage guard delved under the seat and came up holding the treasure chest, leather-bound and padlocked. He balanced it on the grab iron and then let it topple over the side of the coach to land in the dirt with a heavy thud. That startled the bandit's horse so much that it moved back a step or two. The rider settled it with a firm hand on the reins, and he and the guard looked at each other for a long moment.

Something very strange happened then. Griff thought he saw the shotgun guard stiffen, his head lifting sharply. Perhaps the bandit said something, or perhaps Lew Burke read a message in the eyes that met his own. He gave a sudden exclamation; it wasn't loud enough for the passengers over by the creek bank to hear what he said, but to Griff it sounded like a name—a cry that might have been, "Milo! *No!*"

The outcry mingled with the exploding of the gun. To a spurt of smoke and the flat crack of sound across the stillness, Burke was sent backward by the bullet driving into him. It took him in the chest, too ready a target to miss. He dropped in a sprawl onto the seat, like a doll that had been broken and discarded.

The startled teams, still in harness, tossed their heads and tried to stir, but the brake held them motionless. Yonder one of the passengers gave a shocked exclamation. The red-bearded outlaw asked the stage driver in mocking invitation, "You want some of that, maybe?"

His tanned face a shade paler behind his black mustache, Griff clenched his jaw, but he made no answer. And now the one who had put a bullet into Lew Burke snapped an order at his companions: "We have what we came for. Let's get out of here! Fetch the box. . . ."

The one who had been watching the passengers, a huge fellow, rode over and, simply leaning from the saddle, grabbed a handle of the heavy treasure chest. Despite its weight he straightened, with the box dragging from one heavily muscled arm, and he hauled it up across his lap. By now the red-bearded outlaw had joined the others. As they spurred their mounts, he was the one who turned and flung a couple of shots in the direction of the coach, as a last warning.

Then they were galloping away into rocks and pine scrub. Even so, the passengers stayed rooted where they were, almost as though a gun still menaced them. But Griff went into action.

He had to duck past the heads of the lead team as he hurried to snatch up the revolver Burke had tossed into the dirt; he got it and started at a run after the vanished highwaymen, only slowing to a halt as fading hoofbeats made it clear they were already gone past any hope of stopping them.

Left without a target, Griff swore and then wheeled around and strode back toward the stage, the gun swinging futilely in his fist. A confusion of talk had begun among the three passengers, but he shrugged past them and swung up to the driver's seat to check on Lew Burke.

Without even touching him, he knew at once the guard was dead. Griff could only stare at him, his mind a maze of questions. Turning then, he spoke to the men watching him from below. "Did any of you manage to hear what he said, just before that bullet took him?"

All three wordlessly shook their heads. But Griff Connors knew he would never be able to shut out that last, anguished outcry, which he could still hear echoing in his ears: *Milo! No!* . . .

Chapter One

One month after the robbery that had taken Lew Burke's life, Griff Connors sat as a passenger on a stage bound for Leadville, Colorado. So much had happened in one month's time, he reflected, and all because of the robbery—the robbery that he was being falsely accused of participating in by the stage line that had employed him. It seemed strange not to be sitting on the driver's bench, feeling the tug of the teams through the reins. But until he could prove his innocence, his days as a driver were over—and his days as a fugitive from the law had just begun.

Griff thought about the events of the past month that had taken him from Billings, Montana, down through Wyoming to Denver, Colorado, culminating in this stagecoach ride to Leadville. First there had been the robbery, which was bad enough—one guard dead and the bank shipment stolen. When Griff had returned to Billings, he had made a complete statement to the local sheriff and then had gone back to work driving the stage. But then an express company agent, a man named Vern Showalt, arrived in Billings to conduct his own investigation. He decided the holdup had been an inside job and concluded that Griff was at fault; after all, Griff had been the stage driver, and the only other employee on that run had been murdered—hardly the way bandits would treat an accomplice.

When Showalt ended his investigation, Griff had just left on the Miles City run. Showalt, with another stage driver accompanying him to take over the stage run, caught up with Griff at a way station halfway between Billings and Miles City and took him into custody that night, planning to return him to Billings the next morning. Griff repeated his allegation that the shotgun guard had called his killer by name—the name of Milo—but Showalt did not believe him. Realizing a jury would likely concur with Showalt, Griff worked to escape his bonds. Succeeding during the night while the investigator slept, Griff slipped out of the way station, saddled and mounted a horse in the stable, and fled into the darkness.

The luck of the draw had been with Griff that night, for he had several hundred dollars in his wallet, having just been paid for his last two months' work. Throughout the weeks that followed his escape, that money enabled him to visit towns in Montana and Wyoming in search of the outlaw who had cost him his job—and his freedom. Without the money, he would never have been able to induce the patrons of saloons and gambling halls to answer his questions about a red-bearded man who had a large amount of money to spend.

He had tracked the outlaw across the two states, the man's red beard and extravagant spending helping those who had come in contact with the bandit to remember him. Finally, in Laramie, Griff met a woman who knew the robber's name—Ed Luft—and also knew that Luft planned to head to Leadville, to break up a miners' strike, because the stolen money was finally running low. The mineowners in that boomtown were paying good wages to those who would help quell the disturbance caused by the strikers.

Griff sighed aloud. He now had a trail to follow, and although it was a thin one, it pointed to Leadville. He felt sure he could find Ed Luft there . . . but he was also sure that by now Showalt was on his trail. His only hope for exonerating himself was to find the real bandits—and right now his only clue was the man with a red beard.

Griff took a quick glance at the two men sharing the bench with him. They seemed to be traveling together, but neither did much talking. Probably miners, Griff concluded, noting their sturdy builds and heavy work clothes. Leadville was drawing miners like flies to honey, he had heard, and the article he had read in the Georgetown paper while the coach prepared to leave had verified that rumor.

He had read that Leadville, now a city of over sixteen thousand in California Gulch, had mushroomed into being after the gulch had lain stagnant for twenty years, its seven-mile length dotted by only a few straggling camps. Here dogged prospectors had hung on, washing out a little gold, never understanding that the aggravating black sand that hampered their operations was actually carbonate of lead, rich in silver ore. Then overnight the word *silver* had spread, and everything about the area surrounding California Gulch had changed.

The result was predictable. With sudden wealth to be had from the lucky turn of a shovel, fortune seekers of every stripe had poured in, and along with them came the hangers-on and the sharks and murderers, ready to help themselves wherever they saw a chance to prey on likely game. It was easy for a man to go unnoticed there, and Griff had not been too surprised to learn from the woman in Laramie that the redbeard he was seeking might have fled to Leadville.

Griff looked across the stage at the two women passengers seated beside an elderly gentleman. To his way of thinking, the women could hardly have offered more of a contrast, aside from being about the same age—somewhere in their twenties. The taller, dark-haired woman was plainly dressed and subdued in manner. She was pretty enough, in Griff's judgment, with a serious, level look in her brown eyes that he liked. But she had an air of not really being

aware of herself as an attractive female, and so anyone
would have been excused for giving his attention to the
second woman instead.

This one was more than merely attractive. She could
have been called the perfect blond, with the clear, fair
skin, the large and expressive blue eyes, the soft mouth
that went with such a title. Somebody more sophisticated
than Griff Connors might also have recognized that her
traveling dress was expensive and that the golden hair
showing beneath the brim of her bonnet had been wound
around a curling iron in the latest fashion. Griff knew only
that she was extremely pleasing to look at. Although her
conversation was directed at the dark-haired woman seated
next to her, the blond beauty seemed well aware that
every one of the four men who made up the rest of the
coach's passengers was keeping an eye on her. And it
didn't seem to bother her in the least.

Like Griff Connors, yesterday she had ridden the
narrow-gauge railroad west from Denver to Georgetown,
Colorado, and had climbed aboard the stagecoach this
morning for the last leg of the trip to Leadville. It was at
Georgetown that they had picked up the dark-haired
woman, the frail, elderly gentleman carrying a drummer's
case, and the two burly men who sat to Griff's left. Though
the two women evidently were strangers, being thrown
together for a day in a vehicle otherwise filled entirely
with men had led them quickly to develop a friendship. It
hadn't been long before they were deep in conversation,
the blond woman taking the lead.

For a lonely man like Griff, with plenty of troubles on
his mind, the enforced idleness of the swaying, crowded
coach helped him to relax. He enjoyed watching the two
women talk. Without trying to listen to their conversation,
he had learned that the blond woman, who said her name
was Mrs. Elizabeth Doe, was recently divorced after three
years of marriage to the man who had brought her to
Colorado from their hometown in Wisconsin. On her own

now, she was on her way to take a position in a store in Leadville.

The dark-haired woman then told her new friend something of her own biography: "I've lived most of my life in Colorado. Grandpa was one of the pioneers here, in freighting and transportation. My father was killed during the first year of the Civil War when I was just five. Grandpa went to Ohio and brought Mother and me back with him, and I've been here ever since. Ten years ago Mother died, and since then it's just been the two of us."

A little embarrassed at hearing things that were none of his business, Griff reluctantly turned his attention to what lay beyond the window beside him.

There was plenty to see out there. At Georgetown, he had been told that these final sixty miles over the Mosquito Range would be taking them across the very spine of the Colorado Rockies. He could well believe it; he felt as though he were on the roof of the world. The air was thin and chill in his lungs. Griff knew from the way his shoulders were repeatedly thrown against the hard seat back that even though the highest point on the route was already behind them, they must still be crossing rough grade. Yet this new stage and freight road, blasted out nearly twelve thousand feet above sea level a couple of winters ago by two hundred men toiling in subzero weather, was supposed to be easier to travel than the slightly lower route over Weston Pass, which had previously been used by traffic from Denver.

From time to time, above the grind of wheels and creak of leather thoroughbraces and thud of hooves, the driver's voice could be heard shouting at his teams. Griff wondered about him, having a professional interest in his ability. It took heavy wrists and capable hands to manage the ribbons of a six-horse hitch, as he well knew. To Griff's eye, however, the fellow up there on the box might eventually have the build for his job, but now he seemed young for it—hardly more than a kid who had grown too fast, without filling out to match his frame. The young man seemed less than sure of himself, barely experienced enough to be managing an outfit like this one over so rough and difficult a route. What was worse, the horses knew it. Griff wondered just how the young fellow would measure up in an emergency.

He had scarcely had the thought, when he had a chance to find out.

They were hugging the rocky flank of a mountain with a precipitous drop below them, where spires of pine and fir stood straight up like the teeth of a comb. The coach took a blind turn in the road, which was barely wide enough for two vehicles to meet and pass. Without warning, the young driver let out a yell and hauled in his teams, at the same time kicking the brake, and the coach rocked hard on its thoroughbraces, jolting to a halt. The passengers stared at one another, and one of the husky men swore. Griff thrust his head out the window and called forward, "Is something wrong?"

The driver seemed frozen in his place; it took another shout to jar him loose. He wrapped his reins around the brake handle, climbed down from his perch, and came back to peer in at the occupants of the coach, his bony face white. "Road's closed," he announced hoarsely. "There's been a slide."

He had addressed the brown-haired woman. Aghast, she cried, "Oh, no, Jerry!"

"Afraid so." He turned the handle of the door and swung it open. "You better have a look, Nan."

She climbed out, and without being invited, Griff followed. The three of them moved forward, hugging the side of the coach since the drop-off was very near. A glance was enough to reveal the problem. The lead team of the six-horse hitch had been brought to a standstill before a tumble of boulders, where the steep cliff above the road had partially collapsed in a fan of debris that completely blocked half of the road.

The woman named Nan gave a moan of real distress. "But how are we going to get past *that*?"

Jerry Dobbins, the young towheaded driver, said darkly, "With a road as new as this, I guess trouble spots are bound to show up. We've just been lucky something hasn't happened before."

She shook her head. "We have no choice. We'll just have to try to clear it."

"Move all this rock?" Jerry exclaimed. "It would take half a day, even with equipment and a crew!"

"We can't just *sit* here!"

Jerry had no answer for that. They stared at the slide in anguished silence. But then Griff, who had stood apart sizing up the situation—the partially covered roadway, the freshly scarred cliff that rose above it—spoke up. "I don't mean to interfere, but I know of something we might do."

"Yeah?" The young stage driver gave him an unfriendly look. "And who are you?"

"The name's Griff—uh—" He caught himself at the last instant. He felt their eyes on him, and could only hope these two people hadn't noticed the hesitation before he substituted the first name that crossed his mind; he didn't dare take the risk of telling them his own. "It's Griff Cameron," he finished.

The dark-haired woman turned to Griff and told him quickly, "I'm Nan Harper. My grandfather owns this stage."

So that explains her personal concern, Griff thought. He nodded as he said, "Pleased to know you."

She went on seriously, "You really think you have an idea that can help us? We seem a little short of them, just now."

"It all depends on whether you have something on board that can be used for a line. A length of cable, or a stout rope?"

"We do, don't we, Jerry?" she asked the driver, who answered her with a surly nod. She went on to explain, "We always try to carry a rope. In this country, you never know when something can go wrong—for us or one of the other outfits we share the road with."

The driver said belligerently, "So what you got in

mind, mister? There's nothing wrong with my eyesight, you know. There's just no way you or anyone else is going to make the room I need to drive a coach around that rock pile!"

"Take another look," Griff said, pointing up the face of the cliff just beyond the raw scar that had been left when part of the mountain broke loose and spilled down across the road. A single, thick-boled fir tree rose from the rock face, still firmly rooted. "That ought to serve just fine as a place to anchor a rope," he said.

"If I know what you're thinking," Jerry said abruptly, "it can't be done."

Griff corrected him. "I've done it. There's a place down in Arizona Territory where a flash flood ate away more than half a road a lot narrower than this one. We got past."

Nan Harper looked at him quickly. "You've driven stages?"

"Yes, I've driven my share of them. In Arizona—and elsewhere."

"And you're certain this idea of yours will work?"

"I'm sure of it—as long as that tree checks out as solid as it looks." Seeing the questioning look on her face, he went on to explain his plan. First he would separate the two lead horses from the other four—which would remain hitched to the stage—and walk them beyond the rubble in the road. He would tie one end of the rope to their harness, loop the rope around the tree up on the cliff face, and fasten the other end to the side of the coach. When he gave the signal, the two horses on the other side of the slide would pull the rope taut. As the other four animals pulled the coach forward and the left wheels climbed over the rock heap, tilting the coach precariously to one side, the rope would prevent the coach from toppling over the steep drop on the right. If all went well, the coach and horses would pass beyond the rockslide unharmed.

"Too risky!" Jerry pronounced. He gestured toward

the abyss yawning below. "The whole rig is going to wind
up at the bottom!"

Nan Harper pushed a hand through her brown hair as
she looked around. Here they were on the side of a
mountain, with a stalled coach and the ranks of the Mosquito Range marching away into the distance. The thin air
about them was chill despite a bright spring sun shining
off a million rock faces. The rest of the passengers had left
the coach by now and were waiting silently nearby, the
blond woman among them.

The full responsibility for a decision seemed to rest
on Nan Harper. Griff admired the way she faced up to it,
her shoulders stiffening and her jaw setting firmly now as
she nodded to the driver. "You have the final say, of
course, Jerry, but this gentleman's idea makes better sense
than doing nothing." She turned to Griff. "Will you help?"

"Naturally," he assured her. To the driver he said,
"Jerry, fetch the rope and let's see what we've got."

Still scowling, the young fellow went to get it. Griff
told the woman, "If we do make the try, this coach will
have to be unloaded, to lighten it as much as possible."

The rope proved to be heavy, stout hemp, tough and
durable. "We'll hope there's enough." Griff slipped a shoulder through the coils and hoisted their considerable weight.
"Come with me, Jerry," he said. "I want your opinion."

That seemed to mollify the younger man somewhat—
which had been Griff's intention. They walked forward,
skirting the pile of rubble and boulders; it seemed fairly
well settled, and Griff could only hope that their plan
wouldn't cause further sliding. The roadway that remained
clear of the slide would be wide enough for the teams
and—barely—for the outside wheels of the coach. By Griff's
figuring, that ought to be enough.

Beyond the slide Griff found a way to climb up to the
solitary fir tree. As he had hoped, it was stout and well-
rooted enough to serve as an anchor for the line. He took
the rope from his shoulder, gave it a single wrap around

the tree trunk, and tossed one end down to Jerry. The other he flung in the direction of the stalled stagecoach.

While the other male passengers began unloading all baggage and freight from the coach, Griff unhooked the two leading horses and led them past the slide, and he and Jerry improvised a hitch for one end of the rope to the harness. The line's other end Griff fastened securely around a doorpost of the stalled coach. The rope now took the shape of a giant arrow, with its point wrapped around the sturdy fir. To Jerry, waiting beside the two horses on the other side of the rockslide, Griff gave final instructions: "Your job is to keep the horses in their collars and hold the line taut—until I yell at you to give me slack. So keep your ears open, understand?"

"You bet, Mr. Cameron." Impressed by this stranger's apparent confidence in what he was doing, Jerry had lost his earlier belligerence.

The passengers stood in a group, watching in silence as Griff returned to the coach and prepared to mount the front boot. Nan Harper was there, her face a little pale now as she said anxiously, "You'll be careful, won't you? I'd hate to see you taking any risks, on my account."

Griff gave her a grin. "Don't worry, ma'am. I don't intend for anything to happen to me. And far as that's concerned, I want down off this mountain as bad as anyone!"

He rose to his place and gathered the reins of the four horses still harnessed to the stagecoach. The leathers laced themselves into his fingers as though they belonged there. Foot on the brake pedal, he checked everything again— the perilously narrow clear roadway ahead, the sharp drop-off to his right, and above him, the heavy rope slanting away toward the tree trunk to which it was winched. Ahead, almost hidden by a spur of the mountain's flank, Jerry stood waiting with the other two horses.

Griff called out an order, heard the young fellow's shout, and then felt the sharp tug against the coach as the line sprang taut. He drew a breath, kicked off the brake, and yelled at the horses.

They hesitated, waggling their ears. They were reluctant, being only used to working behind a lead team and not liking the looks of what they saw ahead. Griff shouted again and got them into motion. Approaching the slide, where the space for maneuvering sharply narrowed, the horses next to the slide had to crowd farther to their right, and at this their teammates objected, tossing their heads in terror of being forced off the road. As for the coach itself, no matter how close Griff dared to hug the edge, there was not going to be room enough to clear the slide on four wheels.

Suddenly Griff felt the coach stall under him as it struck the edge of the rock pile. He slapped his reins, yelling the teams into their collars. They surged forward. He yelled for Jerry to pull the rope tighter. The left-hand wheels ground over rubble, and then the left side of the coach slowly lifted, and the padded seat of the stagecoach started to tilt under him.

Without warning, the front horse on the right stumbled, then snorted in terror as it tried to rear. Griff's breath caught in his throat; he thought for an instant that all four horses were going to lose their footing and the whole outfit be dragged over the edge to destruction. But he kept a firm hand on the reins, and presently the animals settled. Inch by inch he kept them moving forward.

By this time both left wheels were off the level, struggling over the pileup of boulders and debris and pulling hard against the laboring teams. The coach tilted even higher, and Griff had to fight the slant of the seat or slide off into space. But the line to the tree held, though stretched taut and groaning with the job of keeping the heavy coach from toppling over.

There was an ominous rumbling. The mass of rubble shifted slightly, sending up a cloud of dust and causing the hair on the back of Griff Cameron's neck to stir as he pictured the whole, disturbed mass of rock giving way, snapping the heavy line like a string and sweeping the coach off the side of the mountain. Despite the chill air, he could feel sweat break out on his body and beneath the brim of his hat.

But the moment passed; the horses kept working, straining in their harness. He realized he had gained the midpoint of the slide, leaving more clear road surface ahead. Griff shouted for Jerry to give him some slack in the line. He passed beneath the anchor tree and beyond. Then with a sudden lurch, the near wheels dropped level and the job was done.

Griff pulled in his teams, and only then did his knees grow weak. This had been far more dangerous than maneuvering that washed-out road in Arizona. But he did not reveal any of his shakiness as he wrapped the reins around the brake handle and climbed deliberately down from his place. When he got his boots on the ground, he turned to find Nan Harper there, staring at him, brown eyes wide in a face that was still pale.

"You did it!" she exclaimed, half breathless. "For a moment I thought surely—" Her words stumbled over each other. Impulsively she put out her hand as though to lay it on his arm, but then her natural reserve made her draw it back.

Griff smiled and shrugged. "Glad we found a way out of the problem," he said briefly.

Jerry came running to grab Griff's hand and shake it vigorously. The young fellow was almost dancing in his excitement; any jealousy or resentment of this stranger was completely forgotten. "That took a lot of nerve, Mr. Cameron!" he exclaimed. "But you sure knew what you were doing!"

"Part of the time I wondered if I did," he admitted dryly. "Now we have more work to do—such as getting this coach loaded and the teams back in harness. We must be way behind schedule."

"That doesn't matter," Nan Harper assured him. "It's nothing new for this stage line. I only hope Grandpa won't be worried."

The passengers came straggling up, the men carrying

crates and luggage to load back on the coach. With them was the blond woman, Mrs. Doe, gracefully holding her skirt clear of the rubble underfoot. She walked directly to Griff. Since she was a small woman and he was tall, she had to tilt her head up to one side as she observed him frankly beneath her feathered traveling bonnet.

"Now there's a man with gumption!" she declared. She motioned with the fingers of both hands. "Lean down here for a minute."

"What?"

But she insisted, and after a quick look at Nan Harper he obeyed—to have her place her hands on his shoulders and plant a big kiss on one leather-brown cheek. "There!" She pushed him away and stepped back, then laughed at the flustered look on his face.

Griff wondered if she was making fun of him. Yet strangely enough, he realized what he mostly felt was embarrassment at having Nan Harper see the kiss and hear the blond woman's teasing laughter—and he was a little puzzled to know why a small thing like that should bother him so much.

Chapter Two

Having gained Jerry Dobbins's confidence and respect, Griff accepted an invitation to join him on the driver's seat for the rest of the journey into Leadville. It went without mishap; the horses quickly settled in again to the normal routine, the road proving easily negotiable as they descended the farther slopes of the Mosquitos and the long summer's day began to wane.

Jerry handled his outfit well enough when he wasn't faced with an emergency, but he confirmed Griff's suspicion that he was still fairly new at his job. It appeared that the company he drove for—the Harper Stage Line—was a small one, unable to pay the wages of an experienced crew. "Bill Harper is getting kind of old," the young fellow seriously told Griff. "He's been running transportation here in Colorado longer'n almost anybody, but the years and the competition are beginning to tell. His health ain't been good, either, and doctor bills have taken a lot. Meanwhile you've seen the shape this coach is in. Too much of our equipment's in the same condition. It gets pretty hard to keep things rolling."

"How big a crew do you have?" Griff asked.

"One other man, Dick Walsh. He's a couple years younger than me, and to tell you the truth, we ain't either

19

one of us much to brag about. Both of us are new at this.
And that's just the trouble—Bill can't afford to match the
wages paid by the other outfits that work out of Leadville,
so he can't get experienced workers. And now, since he
lost the mail contract, he has to take what business he can
get."

Griff gathered that, between them, these two green
hands managed to take care of the livestock and keep the
equipment in some kind of running order, as well as
making the Georgetown run three times a week, while
Nan did the bookwork for the company. As a business,
Harper Stage Line was apparently as creaky as the old
stagecoach under them now.

With a resigned shrug, Jerry added, "I guess in a few
more months it won't matter, anyway. All the other lines
will be going out of business, same as this one, once the
railroad hits Leadville."

"When will it be finished?"

"Soon. The Denver and Rio Grande is laying tracks
up the Arkansas Valley right this minute. They and the
Santa Fe had a big fight over who was gonna build the
railroad, but now that's all settled, and there's nothing to
hold 'em back. Everybody knows it's only a matter of time
till they're here and we're out of business. Everybody,"
the young fellow added ironically, "except Bill Harper. He
goes right on pretending it'll never happen. It's too bad,
too." He shook his head. "Bill's a nice old guy, real good
to work for. I feel real sorry for him—and for Nan."

Griff thought about the stage line's problem as they
rolled on, over road that had so recently been blasted out,
with such cost and effort. All that work might soon be put
to naught, through the coming of cheaper transportation.
The price of progress, he supposed.

Presently, after a time of riding in silence, he remarked, "I've heard you have a miners' strike going on in
Leadville."

"Yeah, that's right." The younger man gave Griff a

sharp look. "You wouldn't be one of them that the owners have been bringing in to bust it up?"

"A strikebreaker?" Griff scowled. "That's not my line."

"I hope not," Jerry said gruffly. "The poor bastards that go down into them holes . . . well, *I* wouldn't want to do it, not for the pay they get."

"And how much is that?"

"Just three dollars, for a ten-hour day. Of course," he admitted, "that's more'n I can make, working for Bill Harper. But I've tried it in the mines, and I barely lasted through one shift. Every hour he's down there, a man risks his neck—for the likes of Horace Tabor and Morgan Slaughter and the other mine owners who sit behind their desks and rake in the profits. Ol' man Tabor says the boys down there got nothing to gripe about—claims *he* used to work for three dollars a day and supported a family on it. But hell, that wasn't in no boomtown, like Leadville is now. It costs a man plenty to get by. Anyway, the miners are asking a boost to four dollars, and an eight-hour shift. That works out to fifty cents an hour, and if you ask me they more'n deserve it."

"I'm inclined to agree. Yet the owners are fighting it. . . ."

Jerry vented his feelings by swearing at his horses, which happened to be handy. "Yeah, damn 'em—and using anything they can lay hands on! To date nobody's been killed that we know of, but there's been plenty of hard talk and threats. Some of the strike leaders and a couple of newspapermen who dared to support 'em—they got scared out and left town. Now the talk is that the owners are secretly bringing in an army of toughs and hired guns, and that they'll be sending 'em into action at any minute."

"And you thought I might be one of them?"

The younger man looked embarrassed. "Yeah . . . but you're not the type. I hope you'll forgive my question."

And so they approached the outskirts of Leadville and the tag end of a long day.

The city lay on a long, westward-slanting flat, with
mine workings covering the barren hills that crumpled up
its eastern flank, and mountains raking the far skyline to
the west. Jerry pointed out the two highest in the state of
Colorado, mounts Elbert and Massive, both rising to over
fourteen thousand feet. Griff had heard that Leadville
itself—sitting as it did almost on the very spine of the
Rockies—was the highest organized community in the
entire nation. He could only imagine what this place would
be like in the full grip of a Rocky Mountain winter. Even
now in late May, with shadows lengthening as the sun
dipped toward the silhouette of the western peaks, he was
mighty glad he had the corduroy jacket that covered his
broad shoulders.

Though Leadville's streets were unpaved, Griff could
glimpse evidence of brick construction over toward the
center of town, buildings of two and even three stories
rising above the high facades that lined the wooden
sidewalks—impressive, he thought, for a town that had
hardly existed three short years ago. At the moment,
though, he had little chance to see much of Leadville, for
shortly after the stage wound down from the north and
passed the first fringe of yards and houses, it turned
through a gate in a wooden fence, under a sign identifying
the building inside as the headquarters of the Harper
Stage Line.

"We'll only be here a minute," Jerry told Griff, "and
then I'll run you and the others into town to unload at the
Clarendon Hotel. We're so late that Nan doesn't want to
keep her grandpa worrying. Besides, the sooner she reports that slide, the sooner something can be done about
getting a crew up there to clear it."

The stage yard had seen better days. Griff had learned
earlier from Nan that Bill Harper had been one of the first
to stake his future on the diggings just outside of town in
California Gulch—before there was a town, when a collec-
tion of shacks called "Oro City" had housed prospectors
living mostly on dreams. Harper had freighted supplies for

these diehards. Then when the silver was discovered and prospectors began pouring in, he was the one who sent the first stagecoaches over the passes connecting the boomtown with Denver and the world outside.

But now the lack of business and the threat of unbeatable competition showed their effects on the flagging stage line. The stagecoach came to a halt in a yard whose hard-packed surface was beginning to sprout weeds. Winter snows had caused the roofs of the barn, sheds, and office building to sag. A few head of horses stood, listless, in a corral. A couple of weather-beaten wagons were parked by the fence; there was little else in the way of equipment.

As the coach rocked to a halt, a boy who looked even younger than Jerry came running from the barn. That would have to be Dick Walsh, Griff thought, Bill Harper's yard man—though he hardly looked old enough or big enough to handle the heavy work his job would entail. As Jerry briefly explained their delay to Walsh, the coach door opened and Nan stepped down, along with the drummer and, somewhat to Griff's surprise, the blond woman, Mrs. Doe. He had assumed she would ride the extra blocks to debark at the hotel with the rest.

Apparently not, for he heard Nan giving Walsh orders to get some items of luggage out of the boot. She added, "When that's done, would you mind hitching the buggy, please? Mrs. Doe and I expect to be using it." Griff saw the yard man nod, and when he went to unfasten the leather shield at the rear of the coach, the blond woman and the drummer accompanied him, to identify and claim their belongings.

By now two men had left the office building and were approaching the stage. One had to be Bill Harper, Griff decided. He was frail and elderly, with thinning hair and gaunt cheeks, his movements made uncertain by age and illness. The second man, tall and well built, was a sharp contrast—a man in his forties who appeared prosperous from the cut of his clothing and vigorous with prime good health. He came directly to Nan, and Griff watched him place both hands on her shoulders in a proprietary manner. "My dear!" he exclaimed. "We've been uneasy about you! I knew you were due home today from your trip to Georgetown, and I dropped by, but no sign of you or the stage. Your grandfather was certain something must have happened. Are you all right?"

Griff thought Nan sounded a trifle impatient as she answered. "Of course, Morgan. Everybody's fine."

"Well, thank God for that!" Morgan said, and though she was tall for a woman, he had to bend his head slightly as he kissed her on the cheek.

There was something familiar and possessive about the kiss, and for some reason that irritated Griff. For her part, Nan stood motionless and made no sign of responding. Looking down from his place atop the stage, Griff noticed that even as the man's lips touched Nan's cheek, his gaze had wandered beyond her, to look at the blond woman, Mrs. Doe, who had just accepted a piece of luggage Dick Walsh removed from the rear boot.

Griff frowned. He couldn't blame any man for noticing so attractive a female, yet it didn't seem proper to let it happen while in the act of greeting another woman with a kiss. But it was none of Griff's affair; he shouldn't even have been watching at such a moment, he supposed.

Nan was already turning away from the tall man whom she had called Morgan, disengaging herself to greet her grandfather as he came up to join them.

She gave her news quickly. "Grandpa, we ran into some trouble up near the pass. A slide—a bad one." Alarmed, he wanted to know its location. She told him, concluding, "It all but closed the road, and Jerry and I didn't know how in the world we were going to manage. We'd probably still be sitting up there if we hadn't got some help."

"What kind of help?"

Nan turned and called up to Griff. "Would you mind coming down a minute, please? I'd like you to meet my grandfather."

Griff nodded—he couldn't very well refuse. As he swung off the box, Nan continued her story of the emergency and told of the stranger's suggestion for meeting it. "I was scared at first to let him take the risk, but he seemed to know what he was talking about. As it turned out, he was right."

She made the introduction, adding almost as an afterthought, "Oh, and this is Morgan Slaughter." The tall man gave Griff a crisp nod. He had steely eyes and chiseled features, which held little suggestion of warmth. Griff remembered what Jerry had told him—that this man was one of the owners trying to break the miners' strike and bring them to heel.

Bill Harper said, "We're beholden to you, Mr. Cameron!" The old stage-line owner must once have been at least as tall as his brown-haired granddaughter, but time had shriveled him and hard work had caused his shoulders to sag. Yet the brown eyes that peered up at Griff still held a fierce gleam, and the fingers that closed on his gave a vigorous handclasp. "You done just what I would've in my prime, sir, but Jerry here ain't never come up against a situation like that. I can't fault him for being floored by it." He squinted his eyes as though sizing Griff up and then continued, "This stage line could sure use a fellow with your know-how, if you're looking for a job."

Griff smiled but shook his head. "Thanks. Actually, I'm not."

Bill Harper wasn't prepared to give up so easily. "Right now," he went on, as though Griff hadn't spoken, "I admit we ain't in a position to pay the wages you might get from a couple other outfits around town. But I expect things will be picking up soon."

Griff recalled what Jerry had said about the old man's refusing to admit the railroad coming to Leadville would change things. All he could think of in response was, "I hope you're right. As I said, though, I'm not looking for a job. I'm here on other business."

"We could at least talk about it!" Harper insisted, almost pleading. "Just maybe—"

"I'm afraid not. I'm sorry."

Dick Walsh, having finished buckling the leather shield of the luggage boot in place, called out, "Ready to roll!" And Griff took the welcome chance to break off this conversation. As he turned to climb again to his place, Nan seized his hand in both of hers.

"Mr. Cameron!" she exclaimed. "I don't want you to think there's any reason to apologize. We understand. We're grateful enough for what you did already."

"Glad to help," he said gruffly. As he said it, he happened to glance at Morgan Slaughter, standing to one side, and was startled to see a look of pure malevolence on the tall man's face. Not even when their eyes met did Slaughter make an effort to disguise his naked hostility. Griff figured it was due to the way Nan had impulsively seized his hand and the warmth of her manner toward him.

Griff couldn't be bothered by the mine owner's jealousy, even if it earned him an enemy. For his own part he had already decided he didn't like this man, and he took his time in releasing Nan's hands. He gave her a smile, and then partly to goad Morgan Slaughter, he told her, "If I stay in town for a while maybe you'll be seeing me again."

"That would be nice," she answered.

Deliberately turning his back on the tall man's steel-blue stare, Griff stepped up again to his place on the forward boot. Once he was seated, Jerry yelled at the horses, bringing the coach around in a wide circle, and headed it out the gate, en route to deliver the rest of his passengers to the Clarendon Hotel. The stage-line yard and the people standing in it were quickly swept from view.

As Dick Walsh hurried off to fetch the buggy, Nan watched the stagecoach disappear in a dusty cloud. She then turned to her grandfather and proceeded to introduce her new friend to him and to Morgan Slaughter, explaining, "Mrs. Doe needs a place to stay, but she can't afford the Clarendon. I said I'd show her around. You won't be wanting me for anything just now, will you, Grandpa?"

"No, no," Bill Harper assured her. "You go right ahead. That is, if it's all right with Mr. Slaughter. He did come by specially to see you."

If Morgan Slaughter was disgruntled, he let it go with a shrug. "There'll be another time. I'd better see about sending a crew up there to the pass first thing tomorrow morning and start getting that road cleared. I don't want any more of your runs to be delayed."

"Why, that's mighty kind of you, Mr. Slaughter," Harper said. "I surely do appreciate it."

"No trouble, Mr. Harper. I'll get on it right away."

Dick Walsh rolled up then in the one-horse buggy he had hastily fetched from the barn. He jumped out with alacrity and busied himself stowing Mrs. Doe's belongings, which threatened to overflow the shallow box behind the seat. She thanked him with a smile that fairly dazzled him.

Nan was slightly amused to notice the appreciative look her new friend got from Morgan Slaughter; even her grandfather stood stock-still to watch as the blond newcomer let Dick clumsily assist her up into the buggy. Nan was already in the driver's seat, the reins in her hands. She leaned out to tell her grandfather that she would be back in time to fix supper for them both, and then she and her friend were off.

As the bay horse took them along a side street toward the heart of town, Nan said, "I think I know a very good place for you, quiet and respectable—a boardinghouse, really much nicer and less expensive than you might expect to find in a boomtown like this. I know the landlady, and I'm sure you'll be very comfortable."

"It's sweet of you to take the trouble, Nan."

"No trouble at all. By the way," the brown-haired woman added, "what should I call you? Elizabeth sounds rather formal."

"Back home in Oshkosh, it was always Lizzie—and I hated it. Then after I married Harvey, he had a silly pet name he liked to call me: Baby. Other people took it up, and it stuck. So I guess that's me: Baby Doe! I told you it was silly."

"I like it," Nan protested. "It seems to fit perfectly. Do you mind if I call you that?"

"Why not?" Baby Doe answered with a shrug. "Everybody else does."

The house to which Nan took her friend was a plain wooden building, newly built and unadorned, on a street barren and unpaved like all the others in this raw, new town. The landlady, Mrs. Carlson, managed to keep a few flowers growing in her yard, despite the shortness of the mountain summer. She was delighted to accept Baby Doe as a new boarder and led the way to a little room at the back.

After Mrs. Carlson had left, Baby Doe stood with her luggage at her feet and looked about at the rather sparse accommodations. A brass bed, a crazy quilt covering it, took up most of the space. There was a dresser, a small table, and a couple of chairs; a wardrobe stood in one corner. The center of the floor was covered by a rag rug, and there were curtains at the two small windows.

Feeling some trepidation, Nan reminded Baby Doe, "I warned you it wouldn't be the Clarendon." She poked the mattress on the double bed. "At least you should sleep comfortably."

The blond woman flashed a reassuring smile that showed her dimples. "It'll do fine for now. The Clarendon can wait awhile." She took off her hat and tossed it on the bed, checked her reflection in the dresser mirror, and gave her hair a touch. "Tell me about the Clarendon," she went on as she set about making herself at home. "Pretty nice, is it?"

"I've never been farther than the lobby," Nan admitted. "But I've heard the rooms are beautiful. I've heard stories about how much they cost, too."

"Anything costs that's worth having," Baby Doe observed.

She had opened her luggage and was laying her clothing on the bed, piece by piece, carefully smoothing out any wrinkles. Nan gave a low whistle. "I'll bet they never gave *those* away!"

Baby Doe watched as the other woman touched one of the dresses a little wistfully. "I suppose I went overboard," she confessed. "But it had been so long since I'd had anything new or decent to wear; I was almost in rags, believe me! So, when I got the divorce settlement, I went out and bought the nicest things in Denver. And it was worth every cent, just in the way nice things make a woman *feel*—the confidence she gets knowing she looks her best. I'm sure *you've* found that out."

"Me?" Nan exclaimed, and laughed self-consciously. "A dress like that one would be wasted on somebody like me. I'm just too big . . . and plain, and . . . and awkward. But when someone is beautiful to begin with, like *you*—"

"That's just foolish!" her new friend broke in. She gave Nan an appraising look. "There's nothing at all the matter with you. But it does no good if you keep putting yourself down."

"I don't!" Nan protested indignantly. "I'm just honest with myself."

"If you really think you're all that unattractive, then try to explain the man I saw waiting when the stage got in—the one who kissed you. Who was he, by the way?"

Nan colored slightly. "That was Morgan Slaughter. He owns the Horseshoe mine here."

"Aha! I knew he looked like somebody important. A mineowner—and anybody with eyes could see that you've got him running after you. If you have any sense at all, you'll see to it he catches you."

"Oh, I don't know. . . ." If Nan was deliberately

vague in her answer, it was because she didn't want to discuss with Baby Doe her relationship with Slaughter.

In a way it was flattering—but puzzling, too—that she should have been the one he chose to show an interest in lately. Ownership of the Horseshoe, of course, put him among the elite of wealth and power in Leadville. Perhaps she was too modest, but she couldn't help but wonder what a man like that could see in someone like herself. And, in fact, she wasn't sure she liked his attentions. Slaughter was one of the leaders in opposing the strikers, and they had all of Nan's sympathy in their struggle to win a fair return for their labor in Leadville's silver mines.

Baby Doe pursued her own line of thought as she started to hang her clothing carefully in the wardrobe. "One thing *I* know," she said flatly, "is that I never intend to be poor again—*never*. Look." She turned and thrust out her shapely hands, and Nan saw the ugly calluses on their palms. "You know where I got those?"

"No."

"I'll tell you: hauling timbers and using pick and shovel, right alongside Harvey and our crew. Sinking shafts, working to make the claim that we bought over at Central City pay off. But I didn't mind then; as long as I had faith in my husband, I was happy enough to work with him, even live in a single room over a store. Back home I'd thought Harvey Doe was something special. He had charm, and he was from one of the most important families in Oshkosh. But out here, it didn't take long to learn he had no gumption at all, nothing of what a man needs to make a success. It's a mistake I'll never make again!" she said with conviction. "If I ever take another man, I'll make sure of what I'm getting. My new boss, Jake Sands, is after me to marry him, and he's been a darn good friend; but I can do better than a clothing store owner—even though I'm happy enough, for now, to be taking a job in the store he's opened here in Leadville."

"Oh, is *that* where you're going to work?" Nan exclaimed. "I've seen it. It's a dandy store. Right next to the Clarendon—in Tabor's Opera House."

Baby Doe paused in her unpacking. "Horace Tabor," she said slowly. "*There's* a man I think I'd like to meet! Is he really as rich as everyone back in Denver says? I hear he owns most of Leadville. And now he's the new lieutenant governor of Colorado."

Nan looked at her. "Oh, he's rich all right," she agreed, dryly. "But I used to know him when he wasn't. For years he practically lived from hand to mouth, running a store outside of town in California Gulch. Mrs. Tabor took in boarders to help out. Then one day about three years ago, he grubstaked a couple of prospectors with some canned food and supplies off his shelves, and when they struck it rich on their claim, Horace Tabor was made a full partner. He started with that, and today he owns a lot of other mines and a bank and I honestly don't know what all. He even has his own military society, the Tabor Guard, although everyone knows their real purpose is to march in formation and perform drills. Talk is that he must be taking in at least a million dollars a year."

The blond woman was staring, her beautiful eyes alight with fascinated interest. "And you say you know him?"

"Of course. Everybody in the gulch knew him in the old days. I think he's been around here longer than anyone—even longer than my grandpa. Just tending his store . . . hanging on somehow. Then suddenly lightning struck in the form of silver, and everything changed."

"But the point is," Baby Doe insisted, "when the chance did come, he was ready and knew how to make the most of it. *That's* the kind of man I could be interested in!"

"Well, before you get any romantic notion, I'd better warn you: Horace Tabor must be twenty years older than you. What's more, he has a grown son . . . and a wife."

"Oh." But from the abstracted expression on the blond

woman's beautiful face, Nan found it difficult to tell if she
was listening.

Nan had been sitting on the edge of the bed. A glance
at the window now showed her that the light outside was
fading, as a mountain dusk began to settle over Leadville.
Quickly she was on her feet. "I'd better go. I had no idea
it was so late. The way this town has gotten, Grandpa
doesn't like me out alone after dark." She added anxiously, "You're really sure you'll be comfortable here?"

"After some of the places I've lived in?" Baby Doe
said. "Don't worry!"

"When do you expect to start your job?"

"Tomorrow."

"That soon?" Nan was surprised. "But you only just
got here."

"Listen. Short as I am for money, the sooner I begin
earning some, the better!"

At the door, Nan paused. "Supposing I was to come
by the store, say around noon? The two of us could go out
and have something to eat. I know some good places that
aren't too expensive."

Baby Doe's dimpled smile brightened her face. "That
sounds fine. Let's do it."

She seemed to be sincere; Nan Harper hoped so.
Tooling her buggy homeward through the early darkness,
with Leadville tuning up around her with the raucous
nightlife of a booming silver camp, Nan had to admit that
Baby Doe was different from any other woman friend she
had ever found. She suspected that a number of people
she knew would have their suspicions about a divorced
woman who traveled alone and made no bones as to what
she wanted from life. But it didn't seem to matter.

Nan had to admit she was intrigued by her new
friend. Herself diffident and lacking in self-confidence, she
had a feeling there was much she could learn from knowing the beautiful Baby Doe.

Chapter Three

Aware of the limited money in his pocket and the slim chances of his soon getting any more, Griff Cameron knew without asking that the Clarendon was no place for him—not from his experience with other boomtowns. After the coach pulled to a halt in front of that fine hotel to drop its passengers, he hung back while Jerry Dobbins, the driver, handed out the luggage from the rear boot. Griff accepted his own, exchanged good-byes with the two remaining passengers, and then started off on foot for a look at the town that he had traveled across two states to reach.

The suitcase he carried was no great burden. Aside from shaving materials and a change of shirts, nearly all it contained was his Smith and Wesson .45 revolver and belt holster, along with an extra box of ammunition.

"If you think this place is lively now," Jerry had said, "you should have seen it a couple of months ago, before the strike started!" According to his recital of Leadville's recent history, this city boasted more saloons and gambling houses than any other boomtown—and consequently more outlaws and hustlers.

Griff looked around. Here along the main thoroughfare, as well as on every side street opening into it, flimsily built saloons and gambling halls were crammed cheek by jowl with other, more solid places of business. Pouring from the saloons was a hubbub of sounds—male voices roughened by whiskey, the shrill laughter of women, the occasional racket of a player piano. And this was during the last, slow shank of the afternoon. He could imagine what Leadville would be after nightfall, when things really opened up.

Griff Cameron had little interest in the violent night life of Leadville, except as it might interfere with his purpose—finding the red-bearded man who could prove his innocence. It hadn't been hard to track the bandit to Leadville once Griff had stumbled onto the man's trail. The outlaw had freely spent his share of the loot wherever he went; folks weren't quick to forget a red beard on a man, especially on one going through money so fast.

Griff thought of his own finances. He had to get a room, something between the luxury of the Clarendon and a dollar-a-night flophouse. Afterward, with food of some kind under his belt, he should be ready to sift through this roaring community of Leadville to find the red-bearded stage robber. A day or two, he hoped, would tell him if he had been following a true lead or a dead end.

He was lucky. Only half a block east of Harrison Avenue he found a reasonable hotel, but he paid only for a single night; he had no way to judge how long he might be staying. The second-floor room was small and meanly furnished, its thin walls admitting every sound while trapping in the heat and smells of the day. Griff opened the window to let in some fresh air, and stood a moment looking out across the hotel veranda. Yonder, the whole length of the town's main thoroughfare, Harrison Avenue, was aglow with street lamps, which, Jerry had told him, were lighted with gas from one of Horace Tabor's ventures—a plant to convert coal hauled up from Carson City.

Through the open window, Griff felt a chill wind blow in off the mountains, bringing him the voice of the town. He found himself thinking of the brown-haired woman on the stage. This town was home to Nan Harper—just about the only one she was able to remember, Griff supposed. What would be her future, once the coming of the railroad put her grandfather's stage line out of business? What would become of a frail old man and a simple-hearted girl who knew so little of the world beyond the edges of California Gulch?

Griff shook his head. He had problems of his own to worry about. . . .

Leaving the window, he opened his suitcase and got out a straight razor. He worked up a lather with the bar of yellow soap the hotel provided, and shaved by what was left of the sunlight. Toweling off afterward, he considered what he saw in the uneven mirror: a sun-darkened face, not noticeably handsome, but one he was used to except for one small detail. He frowned as he touched his upper lip, wondering again if the skin there was so much lighter than the rest as to attract attention. Well, too late to worry about it now; the mustache was gone.

He next took out his Smith and Wesson, checked the action, and examined the loads. He shoved the gun behind his belt, on the left side with the handle forward, and then again put on his corduroy jacket, judging that the bulky hang of it should hide the weapon. Satisfied, he took his hat and left the room, locking the door after him.

He found a hole-in-the-wall restaurant where he paid an outrageous price for a slab of burned beef and a few undercooked potatoes. The coffee he could hardly drink. As he was eating he became aware of the talk between two roughly dressed men seated at stools along the counter.

"Then they're going ahead with tonight's strike meeting?" one asked.

"So I hear," the second answered. "Malloy and the others are saying they might as well throw in the towel if they're going to let a bunch of scabs scare 'em into calling it off."

"Where is this meeting supposed to be?"

"Same place as the others—Fryer Hill, about half an

hour from now. There could be some excitement. Think maybe I'll head that way."

"Reckon I will, too."

Working at his tough steak, Griff pondered what he'd heard. The conflict at the mines was, in itself, no concern of his, but he had a good mind to attend this strikers' meeting just in case the man with the red beard was there. He didn't know where Fryer Hill might be, but it would be simple enough to ask . . . or there was an even easier way to find out.

He kept an eye on the pair he'd been listening to, and as they rose to leave, he took a final bite of the steak and washed it down with a swallow of the terrible coffee. He shook his head when the counterman suggested a slice of apple pie; then he tossed money on the counter and followed the two customers out onto the street. When they started to walk east, he unobtrusively fell in several yards behind.

Plainly they weren't the only ones headed for the strikers' meeting. A stream of men was moving along the uneven boardwalks through the rapidly deepening dusk. After a few blocks, the houses thinned out and the ground became rougher; ahead in the fading light a forest of smokestacks rose, marking the higher land above the town, where Leadville's mines covered every inch. Normally, those stacks would be belching smoke, the mines bustling with activity as work continued underground day and night, tearing the rich carbonates from the earth. But now, because of the strike, there was silence. A few lamps burned among the idled buildings where, no doubt, night watchmen would be keeping a vigil against any danger of sabotage.

The strikers were holding their meeting on a barren plot at the lower end of the hill, with Leadville a glowing spread of light below them. Torches had been planted, and a strengthening wind was whipping the flames, casting wavering light and shadow over the men congregated there. Griff had expected a bombastic, fire-eating group, but he saw at once he was wrong. Though there were perhaps two hundred strikers, they were strangely silent; they stood listening to one of their number, a broad-shouldered fellow with the look of an Irishman, who stood bareheaded, his black hair whipping about him in the chill breeze. He had their strict attention, and he wasn't getting it by haranguing the crowd or waving his fists at them. Instead he spoke coolly and calmly, in tones so quiet they scarcely reached to the ring of outsiders who had collected a short distance away to observe what went on.

Griff asked a man standing next to him, "Who's the one doing the talking?"

"Mike Malloy," he was told. "One of the ringleaders. He worked a shift in Slaughter's Horseshoe mine, and he was among the first to walk out. I guess he got a lot of them others to do the same. They all pretty much look up to him."

Even at a distance, Griff could sense something of the black-headed Irishman's strong character—an air of leadership and determination. Obviously Mike Malloy wasn't trying to play on the strikers' emotions—which were already running high—but was soberly discussing the situation. Only a real leader could command such attention from so many obviously angry men. Griff had to respect a man who could do that.

The two hundred men on hand could represent only a fraction of the crews whose massive walkout had closed all those mines. Griff wondered whether more would be coming later or if the rest had been frightened out of attending by rumors of impending violence. He saw no weapons, at least not in the open. Everything about this rally by flickering torchlight seemed peaceable enough.

He was beginning to think the rumors had been no more than a false alarm, when a strident yell suddenly rang across the crowd: "Watch it! *Here they come!*"

They came unhurriedly, deliberately, a solid wedge of figures emerging into the torchlight from the surrounding dusk, each with a red bandanna tied around one arm like a badge. The strikers outnumbered them, but there was something in their appearance that seemed to put the larger group on the defensive. The strikers began to back away until Mike Malloy, holding his ground, was in the forefront as the newcomers came to a halt.

In the lead, facing Malloy, was a solid man, muscular and tough, with a jaw like a shovel. There was contempt in his voice as it pierced the tense stillness. "What about it? You people gonna break this up? Or do you need some help doing it?"

The Irishman, a big enough fellow himself, looked a good many pounds lighter than the man he faced. But his tone was unyielding as he answered with a slight echo of the brogue of his native land, "We'll be needing and wanting nothing from you, Tom Riordan! We're within the law, and within our rights. You can't tell us to break this meeting up."

"No? Well, if *telling* won't do the trick, we got other ways!"

All around Griff there was movement as some of the strikers began to edge back, as though suddenly finding themselves too close to danger. He asked the man next to him, "Who's the loud talker?"

The answer was brief. "Name's Riordan. He works for Morgan Slaughter."

Slaughter again. He seemed to crop up at every turn. "Riordan does his dirty work, you mean?"

The man shrugged. "Calls himself a bodyguard. I guess that can cover almost anything."

Suddenly more men in armbands emerged from out of the surrounding blackness, almost as though a signal had been given, and they closed in on the strikers from two sides, taking them by surprise. All at once there was a confusion of flailing arms and yells and a scuffle of boots, and the battle began.

Those men who had come to the meeting only out of curiosity were scrambling now to get away, and Griff was nearly overrun. Staggering, he shoved aside those who blundered into him. His hand slipped under his jacket and closed upon the butt of the Smith and Wesson; still, this was not his fight, and he saw no reason for mixing into it.

Then amid the streaking dust and torchlit shapes of struggling men, he had a single, brief glimpse of a face that froze in his mind like a photograph. It was contorted in anger, the mouth open on a shout—and covering the chin were wiry, reddish whiskers. A moment later the face was lost in the milling press, but it had sprung Griff loose as though he had been hurled by a catapult. He lunged forward, the pistol now in his hand.

It was mostly a silent battle, clubs against fists; only twice was it punctuated by gunshots. Trying to break through the crowd, he found himself confronted by a man wearing a red rag around his arm, holding a heavy plank, which he immediately swung. Griff braced himself and flung up a hand, managing to catch and deflect the other's arm and abort the clublike blow. Taking advantage of the man's surprise, Griff clipped him sharply alongside the head with the barrel of the Smith and Wesson and saw him fall.

Not giving him a second look, Griff began to charge ahead, hunting for another glimpse of the red-bearded man. It was then that something struck him across the back of the skull, causing an explosion of stars, and then all the stiffness went out of his legs and he dropped, prone, atop the man his own gun barrel had felled.

He didn't think he had lost consciousness, but he must have. When he tried to raise up from the cold ground, the smell of blood hung in his nostrils, and a throbbing ache filled his head. Griff realized he had been moved, since the body he had fallen on was gone. The melee seemed to be over; in its wake, stillness lay across Fryer Hill. After a moment Griff flattened his hands against the chill ground, gritting his teeth against the pain in his skull, and pushed himself to his knees.

Many of the torches had gone out or been thrown down, but a few still burned in place. By their wind-whipped and scattered light he stared around at the site of the recent battle.

He expected to see bodies littering the ground or men moaning with the pain of broken heads, but there was little evidence of that kind to show the fight had taken place. The combatants had either fled or been carried away. Griff saw the dull glimmer of his own gun, lying where it had fallen. Feeling momentarily stronger now, he struggled to his feet and went to pick it up. The throb inside his skull seemed to ease a trifle as he moved around. His vision seemed to be all right, with no hint of double image, and he decided he couldn't be too seriously injured.

Then, some distance from where he stood, a torch that still burned where it was thrust into the ground illuminated two men hovering anxiously over a third, who lay motionless between them. One of the two turned his head, and in the flickering light Griff recognized Mike Malloy, the strike leader. On impulse Griff slid his revolver behind his belt and began to walk toward Malloy, growing steadier with each step he took.

Engrossed in their own concerns, Malloy and the other man didn't notice Griff until he was almost upon them. Suddenly the man standing with Malloy jerked his head around, and his right hand dived into his coat pocket and brought out a snub-nosed revolver. Griff halted in his tracks as its muzzle settled on him.

"Stop right there!" said a strained and dangerous voice. "I don't know you!"

Griff quickly raised his hands. "You wouldn't. I'm new in town—just got in this evening." He indicated the hillside where the battle had raged. "I had nothing to do with this."

The black-haired leader had been studying him. He told the other man, "He's wearing no armband, anyway." Suddenly his expression took on a new interest. "Wait a minute! Sure, an' I think I seen you poleax Rufe Schults during our little donnybrook. He's one of the worst of that crowd; I'd say you must be on our side." He extended his hand to Griff and added, "My name's Malloy."

"I know," Griff lowered his arms and shook the hand the Irishman offered him. "If I'm on anybody's side, I guess it's yours. But actually, there's a couple of questions I wanted to ask."

"Ain't a time for jabber," Malloy's companion objected bluntly. He had lowered his gun, and he used it to indicate the figure lying on the ground. "This man's been knifed, and my damned arm is broke where some son of a bitch used a club on me!" That explained the hot look in his eyes—it was simply pain, enough to have made anyone short-tempered and difficult. He added, "We got to clear out before the town marshal gets wind of the trouble and comes up here and starts arresting anyone he sees!"

Looking more closely at the fallen man, Griff now saw by the flickering torchlight the slack features and blood-soaked clothing. "I'll give you a hand with him."

"Thanks—we can use one," Mike Malloy said. "I'll be more than glad to hear your questions once we get him to my shack—and do something about Frank's arm."

"It's a deal," Griff said.

Chapter Four

Mike Malloy's home was little more than a hovel. It was located in a poor district, inhabited by the workers who toiled to dig wealth from the earth for Leadville's powerful mine owners. Malloy's shack was a bleak place of two small rooms and a loft where his two children slept, but it was neat as a pin and made cheery by a blaze in the open fireplace. Malloy's wife, as Irish as himself, met them at the door, a look of alarm on her rosy-cheeked face.

She had probably heard news of the trouble at the meeting, but she spent no time on questions after a swift glance assured her that her man was safe. She held the door wide as he and Griff brought in the hurt man, whom Malloy called Vince, and then she shooed her children away and cleared a bed for him. A lamp was brought and the knife wound quickly laid bare. The blade had sliced across the man's ribs, and he had been bleeding freely. "Where can I get a doctor?" Griff asked.

Malloy shook his head without pausing in his examination of the wound. "Why, a doctor ain't necessary. It's a clean wound, nothing that Mary can't tend to all by herself. Ain't I right, Mary?"

"La, yes!" she exclaimed emphatically.

"One thing you *could* do," the Irishman told Griff, "is go out there and give Frank Gower a drop of the old stuff. I think he can use it about now with his arm causing him such pain."

"All right," Griff said. He returned to the main room where the man with the broken arm was seated at the table, looking glassy-eyed now as the shock of pain got to him. Griff found glasses and a bottle on a shelf, took the whiskey to the table, and poured a stiff drink, which Gower tossed back as though scarcely aware of what he did.

Presently Malloy joined them. He answered Griff's question with a nod. "Vince is gonna be all right. He'll walk around bent over for a while, until things start to mend. For now we'll see that he stays where he is." He gave Griff an appraising look. "You appear a brawny sort of lad. Maybe you can give me a hand here." He indicated Gower with a movement of his head.

"Glad to. Whatever I can."

"He better have another jolt of this in him." Malloy poured the glass full again, and the hurt man mechanically drained it. From the tinderbox by the fireplace, Malloy selected two slivers of pine and brought these to the table, along with a piece of toweling. Then he gestured for Griff to come around behind Gower's chair and silently indicated what to do. The broken arm lay upon the table, and Malloy gently unbuttoned the shirt cuff and slit the sleeve away with a knife. The skin had not been broken. Malloy studied the unnatural bend between the wrist and elbow of Gower's arm.

He said quietly, "Now!"

Griff put both hands on the man's shoulders, and Malloy seized the arm at wrist and elbow and gave a deft, quick pull. The sound of the broken bones grating into place was distinctly audible; Gower made a convulsive lunge, but Griff was ready and held him firmly in his chair. Then Mike Malloy had the splints in position and was methodically wrapping the cloth to hold them.

The job finished, the Irishman said gruffly, "I think I could use a jolt of that stuff myself!"

The inevitable letdown followed. Malloy had his drink, and they sat in stillness except for the snapping of the fire, the sounds of Mary Malloy going about her work, and the subdued whispering of the children, who had been sent up to the loft. Gower, his arm resting in a sling, was subdued and pale after his ordeal.

They seemed to have accepted completely the man who called himself Griff Cameron. He asked them now, "What do you figure this business tonight is going to cost you?"

"Nothing at all, far as I'm concerned," Malloy answered. "All it does is show that the owners will stop at nothing to try to break us. That means that the strike must be starting to hurt them. It's no time to be thinking about quitting."

"Are you sure some of your people aren't losing their nerve? Seemed to me it was kind of a sparse turnout for your meeting. Having it broke up might discourage them even more."

"I've got to believe it'll do just the opposite," the Irishman said stoutly. "True enough, some have started to lose heart—it ain't easy to make ends meet, especially if you got a family to feed and no money coming in. But wait till they get word about tonight! We knew about those toughs being brought in, but a lot of the boys just didn't want to think that old Horace Tabor would actually let 'em be used against us. Well, now they're going to know different. And I'm guessing it's going to make them madder than hornets!"

"Somebody told me the one who led the raid doesn't work for Tabor," Griff noted.

"Tom Riordan? He's Morgan Slaughter's man," Gower confirmed, his voice grim. "And it's Slaughter who calls the shots and keeps Tabor and the other owners holding the line firm at three dollars a day."

"I worked at Slaughter's Horseshoe mine," Malloy added bleakly. "The trouble really began when he let it be known he was fixing to cut salaries to two dollars and seventy-five cents. A man can't feed his family on that kind of money! That's when we decided we didn't have no choice but to close down the mines. And because I was one of the first to call for a strike, I've been a marked man ever since."

"Show him the letter," Gower suggested.

Malloy dug a folded paper from his shirt pocket and passed it across the table to Griff. "I found that under my door, just this morning."

Unfolding it, Griff read the brief, neatly written message:

> Sir:
>   You are hereby ordered to leave Leadville by noon tomorrow, to be seen no more. Disregard this notification at your peril.
>   By order of the
>   Committee of One Hundred

Malloy said bleakly, "I was beginning to wonder when it would be my turn for one of these."

Griff flicked the paper with his thumbnail. " 'Committee of One Hundred.' That sounds impressive, but it doesn't really tell you anything."

Gower gave a snort. "You can figure at least ninety of 'em are Morgan Slaughter. Not that anyone can prove it."

"And what happens to the man who gets this and refuses to leave?"

"Up to now," Malloy said, "nobody has."

Something in his tone caught Cameron's glance. "Up to now?"

The Irishman lifted his head. He looked about him, at the impoverished but homey interior of the shack, at his wife, who stood silently listening in the bedroom doorway, at the opening to the loft, where his children now slept. He said slowly, "I'm not going. The boys have followed me into this thing. I'll not walk out on them!"

His words hung in the stillness. Griff Cameron, handing the letter back, said quietly, "I had an idea that's what you would tell me."

The mood changed. The black-haired man shoved the paper away into the pocket of his shirt as he said abruptly, "So much for that. . . . Now wasn't there something you wanted to ask? Ask away—sure an' we'll tell you anything we can."

Griff drew a breath. "There's a man I'd like to know about—he's the reason I'm here in Leadville. I think I saw a glimpse of him tonight, up there on Fryer Hill. He helped Tom Riordan bust up your meeting—fellow with a red beard. I was trying to get to him when somebody laid me out. Does the description ring a bell?"

The other two exchanged a quick glance, and Malloy said, "Could be. Lately, you can imagine we've kept our eyes peeled for strangers who could be strikebreakers. They got a hangout down on State Street, and we try to watch them as they come and go. Unless I'm mistaken, a fellow like that showed up there for the first time just a day or two ago."

Gower added, "I know the one. Red beard; mean-eyed sort. I think I heard a handle for him, too. Taft, or something that sounded like that."

"Would it have been Luft? Ed Luft?"

"By God, I think that was it!"

Griff was already on his feet, leaning for the hat he'd dropped to the floor beside his chair. "This hangout you mentioned. On State Street, you said?"

"It's called Drago's—a gambling hall." Malloy looked concerned. "You best be careful, if you go nosing around down there. It's a tough dive, on the worst street in town."

"I figure to watch my step."

But suddenly he was reluctant to go; there seemed more that needed to be said. He told Gower, "I hope you mend all right—and your friend in the other room. If I don't see any of you again, I wish you all the best of luck.

I'm only an outsider, but in your place I think I'd do
exactly what you're doing."

Mike Malloy, rising also, offered his work-toughened
hand. "We appreciate your help this evening."

Griff said pointedly, "I hope you'll be walking careful,
come noon tomorrow." Moments later he was gone.

Though most of Leadville's business houses were still
illuminated by kerosene, the glow of the newly installed
gas street lamps turned the entire length of Harrison
Avenue into a broad canyon of light that dimmed the stars
overhead. State Street, near the foot of Harrison, lay only
a block south of the elegant and brilliantly lit Clarendon
Hotel and Opera House.

By contrast, State Street was more like an unlighted
alley, crowded cheek by jowl with bars, gambling dives,
and worse. Griff instinctively felt for the butt of the Smith
and Wesson as he walked along and saw dim figures
moving in and out of shadows. Drago's, identified by the
name stenciled on the glass of a lighted window, lay well
along the first block west of Harrison. He halted and
positioned himself so he could get a look inside.

It was no better than the other dives, with a plank bar
and plain chairs and tables for gambling. Drago's was
busy, and Griff thought the crowd seemed to be celebrating—perhaps celebrating the successful routing of the miners' meeting earlier that night. He hunted the faces for
Tom Riordan and for the red beard of Ed Luft, but he saw
no sign of either. Disappointed, he decided to withdraw
from the window before he became conspicuous. He drifted
across the street into the shadow of a darkened building,
where he was able to watch the entrance to Drago's and
observe anyone who went in or out.

Whenever the door opened, enough light spilled out
to give him a good look at the person entering or leaving.
But time passed, and he saw no one that fit Luft's description. Presently he found his attention drawn to a spill of
light against the wall of a neighboring building, from the
window of what could be a private gaming room toward

the rear of Drago's. Even as he looked at it, that light went out as though the game might have broken up. It seemed to make no difference in the sporadic flow of traffic out of the gambling hall.

The chill of the high Rockies grew more pronounced as the night grew older. So also, if anything, did the raucous voice of State Street. With it came the realization that he had been standing here too long, and that his presence had surely been noticed. Better not to press his luck by rousing suspicion. After all, he told himself, he'd accomplished a good deal more in his first few hours in this town than he would have had any right to expect. He definitely knew now that Ed Luft was here; he had even seen him. He felt that all the work he had done to get to Leadville was worth it, and he could make do with that, for one evening.

With a strong sensation of being watched, he turned his back on Drago's and State Street. Late as it was, Leadville showed no signs of quieting down; if anything the night was only gathering steam. But the letdown after days of hard travel, and after the last eventful hours, suddenly weighed upon him. By the time Griff reached his hotel, got the key, and climbed the steps to his room, he had begun to understand how dog-tired he actually was.

A methodical person by nature, he laid jacket, shirt, and trousers on the seat of a chair, placed his gun in easy reach on top of them, and arranged his boots neatly under the bed. Then he extinguished the lamp and stretched out, listening to the night sounds of Leadville through the open window.

He didn't know how long he had been asleep, but it could hardly have been for long, when a new sound roused him. Griff lay there listening, and when it came again, he knew what he had heard was the creak of a floorboard just outside his door. He stretched out an arm, found the butt plates of the Smith and Wesson, and silently picked it up. He waited.

Metal scraped faintly as someone cautiously tried the knob. Finding the door locked, whoever was out there hesitated for the length of a breath; then, just as cautiously, the knob was released.

Instantly Griff came up onto an elbow, bringing the gun around to where a faint line of light outlined the ill-fitting panel along the edge of the jamb. Once more the board creaked, and Griff knew the one who had tested the knob of his door was retreating.

Flinging the covers aside, he swung off the bed, reaching for and slipping into his trousers. Holding the gun, he padded barefooted across to the door, found the key in the lock, and turned it. The door sprang open, revealing the corridor, lit by the faint glow of a wall lamp, lined with closed doors. The dead air of the hallway held the musty smell of dust and the muffled sounds of sleeping persons.

From the stairwell came the faint echo of footsteps quickly descending and then crossing the lobby below. Griff ran to the stairs, but by the time he reached a point where he could peer into the lobby, it was empty. The door stood open to the dark street outside; there was no one on duty behind the desk, no one who might have seen the prowler leaving. Griff drew a breath.

He was thinking again of that sensation he had had, while waiting across from that dive on State Street, of unseen eyes resting on him. Supposing that had been something more than imagination and taut nerves? All at once he felt a new conviction that Ed Luft was aware and watching him—could even have followed him to his hotel room, to try the door and find it locked. . . .

As he turned back to his room, he felt the beginning of anger at work in him.

Chapter Five

By daylight Griff Cameron had all but convinced himself that the hand that tried his door last night could have belonged to any petty thief looking for a room to ransack or perhaps a place to flop. But it was an alarming thought that the man he was hunting might have reversed procedures and begun stalking Griff instead.

If that should be true—if Ed Luft really had spotted him and followed him to his room—then he was a marked man. It was always best to carry the fight to an enemy, rather than give him the chance to strike first.

Griff considered his problem over breakfast—to all outward appearances unconcerned but actually burning with growing irritation. By the time he finished and left the restaurant, he had come to a decision. He would not wait for Ed Luft to hunt him down; he would take the offensive.

He had been in mining towns before, and as he walked in the crisp sunlight along Harrison Avenue he could see how the strike had nearly paralyzed this one. No ore wagons rumbled through the streets. The tall smokestacks on the heights east of town were idle. There was no huff of donkey engines hoisting work crews up and down the shafts, no rumbling of dynamite blasts deep in the earth. Instead, men who should have been down there now, toiling underground, merely swelled the idle throngs that filled the streets of Leadville, keeping the saloons and gambling dives going around the clock.

Once more Griff Cameron made his way to State Street, but this time, on arriving at Drago's, he boldly pushed open the door and entered. The room was about half full, and there was no sign of a man with a red beard. Griff walked over to the counter and signaled the bartender.

The unshaven man approached him with an unfriendly look, well aware that this was not one of his regular customers. Griff ordered a beer. As it was pumped and collared and shoved across to him, he knew that the denizens of the place were giving him careful and suspicious attention.

He took a drag at the beer and then set it aside. Making no attempt to keep his voice down or prevent the patrons from hearing, he asked the man behind the counter, "Would the name Ed Luft mean anything to you?"

Before answering, the bartender gave a couple of swipes at the wood with the bar rag. "Should it?" he grunted. "I hear a lot of names."

"If he comes in, I'd like you to pass him a message. All right?"

"Maybe." The man shrugged elaborately. "If he comes in. What's the message?"

"Tell him I'm tired of beating around the bush. If he thinks he has business with me, he'll find me at the hotel. I don't think I have to tell him which one."

The bartender went through a ritual of unfolding his rag, finding a clean place, and refolding it. The room was nearly silent when he demanded, "Who am I supposed to say I heard this from?"

"Luft will know," Griff answered coolly. "But tell him I don't intend to wait forever." He took a coin from his pocket, laid it on the bar, and pushed coin and glass across the damp wood toward the other man. "I've been served

better beer than that," he commented dryly. Then he
turned and walked out.

The hotel had a veranda fronting the street, lined by
a row of chairs. Griff mounted the steps, picked a chair,
and let himself into it. Idleness went against his grain, but
having thrown out his bait, he had no choice but to wait
and see if Ed Luft would rise to it, if only out of curiosity.
Griff tried not to grow impatient.

Someone had left a newspaper next to his chair, and
he made himself comfortable while he gave it a leisurely
reading, right through the local news and the advertise-
ments to the syndicated news that filled up its inside
pages. Two things caught his notice. First was the amount
of space devoted to crime and violence. If there was any
doubt that Leadville was a wild and tough town, all one
had to do was count the number of local shootings, stab-
bings, and incidents of general mayhem recorded from the
previous week. Secondly, the bias in its editorials about
the miners' strike made it clear that the *Carbonate Weekly
Chronicle* was solidly on the side of the mineowners and
of the powers that ruled this town.

So much, he thought, for fair and impartial coverage
in the local press. Mike Malloy and his friends could look
for it in vain.

Done with the paper, Griff laid it aside, rolled a
cigarette, and struck a match on the underside of the
chair. Afterward he braced a boot against the railing and
settled back, to all appearances a man with nothing better
to do than idle away the morning, taking things easy while
he watched the flow of life passing in the street. No one
would be likely to notice his slow deepening of tension as
time passed and he began to wonder if his message to Ed
Luft would bear fruit.

The sun stood high, and traffic in this sidestreet picked
up some with the approach of noon. A buggy came rolling
toward Harrison Avenue, and Griff realized that the person perched on its leather seat was Nan Harper.

She looked very attractive, he thought, when not

placed in contrast with the petite loveliness of the beautiful Mrs. Doe. The dark-haired woman seemed not at all awkward, in fact quite the opposite as she handled the reins and guided her horse through the traffic. She noticed Griff and lifted a hand in greeting. Waving back, he saw she was pulling the bay horse to a stop; she seemed to want to speak to him.

Griff left his chair and dropped down the steps, removing his hat as he came toward her. "Good morning," he said.

"Good morning!" she returned brightly. "How are you?"

"I've nothing to complain about."

"I'm glad." But having said this much, she hesitated. She looked down at her hands, which held the reins. He waited, and she raised her head with a sober look as she blurted suddenly, "Mr. Cameron, I want to apologize."

He stared. "Apologize? Whatever for?"

"For yesterday," she answered, "when we got in to the station. I am terribly sorry about the way Grandpa acted. Oh, I knew he'd probably offer you a job with us—only he wouldn't let it go at that! Even when you said no, he kept right after it, almost *begging* you! I could see how hard you were trying to find an answer without hurting his feelings."

"It's perfectly all right," Griff said. "There's certainly no reason for an apology. I was sorry to disappoint him by turning him down. But there were reasons why I couldn't say yes."

"I understand that. I only hope you can understand about Grandpa—how anxious he is about things, just now. You see, he thinks if he had someone of real experience working for him, it would make all the difference. Jerry and Dick try hard, but there's an awful lot they just don't know. I'm sure you looked like the answer to all his problems."

"I'm not sure there is any answer," Griff said. "Not if it's true you're about to get competition from the railroad."

A troubled expression darkened her eyes. "Oh, it's true enough. We've known it a long time. But I think Grandpa deliberately shuts his mind to it, simply refuses to admit the facts. Because once the railroad's completed, not only ours but every other stage and freight line operating out of Leadville is going to be put out of business. And he just can't bring himself to face that."

There was such a genuine feeling for the old man's predicament in every word she spoke that Griff could only share her sympathy. In the end all he could say was, "And what will *you* do, Nan?"

She didn't seem to notice that he had called her by her first name; there was something so open and frank about her that it seemed the natural thing to do, even after such short acquaintance. She answered seriously, with a little shake of her head, "I don't really know. This stage line has been Grandpa's life. I don't like to think what it might do to him, if the time comes that he has to give it up." But then, with a clear effort, she forced a smile and a lighter tone. "Oh, well. We have some time yet. Something will turn up."

"I very much hope so," he told her sincerely. "I wish you both only the best."

"Thank you." She lifted the reins as she added, "And I wish you the same, Mr. Cameron. . . . I have to go now. I'm supposed to meet my friend, Mrs. Doe."

She smiled and gave another nod, and she was gone. Griff watched her horse and rig move down the hill away from him, turning at last into the traffic on Harrison Avenue. It seemed to him a little odd that the acquaintance struck up between the two young women on the coach yesterday could develop into friendship. They were so different—the rather flamboyant blond beauty and this quiet, dark woman, self-effacing in her modesty. Still, they seemed very nearly of an age, and in a town like this one it might not be easy for Nan to find a friend of any kind that she could feel comfortable with.

But then he shrugged, remembering what he was

doing here. It was close to noon, the morning gone while he waited for Ed Luft to answer his challenge. He would give the man another half hour. Doggedly, he climbed the steps again to the veranda and resumed his place, tilting back the chair and pushing his hat over his eyes to shade them. Though he appeared to be dozing, beneath the brim his glance was busy and alert.

Yet when someone finally stopped beside his chair, he was taken by surprise. He had heard no footsteps. One of the floorboards of the porch had creaked faintly, and then he had sensed a man standing over him. Reacting instantly, he let the chair legs drop sharply as his head jerked up and he reached toward the gun under his jacket. But he checked the movement when he saw Mike Malloy staring at him with startled eyes.

"Hey!" he exclaimed, and drew quickly back. "I didn't mean nothing, Cameron. I thought you might be asleep. I didn't want to rouse you if you was."

Still feeling the sudden surge of adrenalin, Griff shrugged and batted the hat back from his face. "It's all right," he said gruffly. "Maybe I did doze off for a minute."

"Sure, an' I guess it ain't always safe to sneak up on somebody!" Malloy appeared to be shaken. "I bet I'll never do that again!"

Before Griff could answer him, they heard through the hotel's open door the clock in the lobby chime a single stroke. It reminded him of the anonymous letter he had read in Malloy's cabin. "An hour past noon," he remarked. "No trouble yet?"

"None yet," Malloy replied. But Griff observed how warily the Irishman glanced into the sunlit street. Now Malloy lowered himself into a chair; though he stretched his legs in apparent relaxation, he was clearly more on edge than he cared to admit. "You can see I didn't leave." He touched the pocket of his shirt. "I've got the letter right here, and I'm calling their bluff. Now it's up to them."

"Then you really think it's a bluff?"

"I'm still alive, ain't I?"

"Looks to me what you're doing is setting yourself up as bait."

The Irishman snapped his head around. "Would you expect me to hide?" he demanded. "Stay holed up in that shack till they come for me—with my family right there and all? No, damn it! If they want to take me, it'll have to be out in the open—where the whole town can see!"

Griff had no answer for that. Obviously Malloy was grimly determined to stay with the course he'd set—and it was his decision to make. The Irishman abruptly changed the subject. "Reason I stopped by was to find out if we were any help last night, finding the man you were looking for?"

"Luft?" Griff shook his head. "I went to the place on State Street but didn't see him. But I'll keep after it." He saw no point in mentioning the incident at his hotel room since he wasn't certain who had tried his door. "What about your friend who got knifed? How's he doing?"

"All right," Malloy said. "My Mary is a first-class nurse. Vince was feeling pretty frisky when he woke up this morning."

"Glad to hear it. A knife cut can be tricky."

"Yeah." Suddenly the Irishman was on his feet again, propelled by the tensions at work in him. "Well, this ain't getting me anyplace!" he said gruffly. "I'm thinking I'll go down on the avenue. If anything does happen, I'm gonna want lots of people on hand to see it."

Griff rose as well. "A lot of other men are letting their futures ride on your shoulders. Shouldn't some of them be here to back you?"

Malloy shook his head emphatically. "Then I'd be *asking* for a fight—and a fight ain't what I want. No, I got to do this alone."

"Then good luck to you."

Griff frowned as he watched the other man step easily down the hotel steps and make his lonely way down the hill toward Harrison Avenue—a solitary figure, facing an uncertain situation. Malloy was a brave man, working for a cause he felt was just; Griff couldn't help but feel sympathy, even if it was no direct concern of his.

Suddenly he stiffened. Farther up the street a man had left the shelter of a doorway where he had been standing motionless, watching. Now he was walking this way, and Griff knew at once that Malloy was being followed. Stepping into the shadow of the wooden roof, Griff brought the gun out from under his coat.

As the man drew nearer, it was evident he wore a holstered gun. Then Griff saw his face—hard-eyed, unshaven—and recognized it as one he had glimpsed last evening at Drago's. That settled it. He let the man come even with him. Then he stepped clear of the pillar and said sharply, "Hold it where you are!"

In midstride the man halted and jerked his head around. He stared at the gun trained on him, and by reflex his hand began a move toward his own holster before he checked it. He blurted harshly, "What the hell is this?"

Griff told him in a mild tone, "Why, to me it looks like somebody is tailing a man—maybe with the idea of killing him. How does it look to you?"

From the flickering of the stranger's expression, Griff knew he had struck home. The man's jaw bulged as he clenched the muscles, and he spoke a taut warning: "I'd say *somebody's* trying to mix in things that ain't his business! And he's likely to be sorry."

"You don't scare me much," Griff retorted. His voice hardened as he added, "Let's see you take out that gun and lay it on the step here in front of me."

"Like hell!" came the reply, but then the steely-eyed man gave another look at the Smith and Wesson pointed at his head. Griff's cold stare seemed to caution the man. Swearing, he tossed back the skirt of his jacket, gingerly lifted the revolver from its holster, leaned over, and placed the weapon on one of the wide plank steps.

"Good! Now move away from it," Griff Cameron ordered.

Disarmed, the man obeyed. He stood glaring as he waited to learn what would happen next.

Griff didn't make him wait long. "I want you to turn around and head back where you came from," he said, wagging the barrel of the gun suggestively.

The other man shot a glance in the direction Mike Malloy had gone. Then he turned his hard stare back to Griff and said harshly, "That's all right . . . they know he's coming. I was only supposed to see that he didn't turn back."

"*You're* the one that's turning back," Griff told him. "Now!"

No longer arguing, the man gave Griff a last furious stare, swung around, and started tramping away in the opposite direction, his boots knocking angrily against the boards of the sidewalk. When he was gone, Griff Cameron stepped down from the veranda, leaned over, and caught up the captured weapon.

He looked around. The scene had been played on such a low key no one had even noticed it. Even so, Griff felt a very real sense of alarm.

Although Mike Malloy knew he was most likely in danger, he did not know where the threat was coming from. And now he was actually being stalked through the streets of Leadville. His enemies had only been biding their time, waiting to make absolutely certain that he was defying the letter that had ordered him from town. And at this moment he was walking into their trap.

Griff made a sudden decision. Not having any need for the captured gun, he tossed it far back under the hotel porch steps. Then he started down the hill, listening for a sound of gunfire.

Chapter Six

After she pulled up her buggy at the curb and hopped down to fasten her bay horse to the hitching post in front of Tabor's Opera House, Nan Harper paused to gaze at the ornate brick building that rose above her. Three stories high, fronted by tall windows and with a balcony over the main door, it towered above all the rest of Leadville.

It was a sight that never failed to excite her, even though more than six months had passed since its grand opening last November. She admired the building's solid architecture, the gold letters in bas-relief above the second story front that identified it. The very name suggested the wonders within; so did a glimpse into the lobby, where an elegant staircase swept one in imagination up to a set of double doors and the auditorium beyond.

Having waited in mounting excitement as she had watched the theater being built, Nan had thought her heart would break when she wasn't allowed to attend that November opening. The night before, two men had been lynched in an unfinished building across the street, and Grandpa had put his foot down, declaring this lower end of Harrison Avenue to be no safe place after dark for a respectable young woman. Afterward, though, he had relented, and they had attended performances together half a dozen times through the long winter; the old man had enjoyed them almost as much as she did herself.

Next door to the Opera House, and also due to the enterprise of the wealthy Horace Tabor, Leadville's other showcase stood—the Clarendon Hotel. A covered walkway had been installed connecting the upper stories of the two buildings, giving the hotel's well-heeled guests a way to get from their rooms to the theater without having to face bad weather outside. As Nan had told Mrs. Doe, up to now she had ventured no farther than the lobby of the hotel. But she had heard descriptions of expensive suites and their furnishings that fascinated and intrigued her. Like the magical performances on the stage of the Opera House itself, the fabulous Clarendon seemed to speak of a world far different from the one she knew.

Nan gave the bay horse a pat on its nose and turned to enter the Opera House.

On the ground floor, to either side of the main entrance, a couple of business establishments fronted the busy street. The one on the north was a clothing store, with the name "Sands and Pelton" displayed on the plate glass windows. Nan entered, stepping into an atmosphere redolent of newness, of fresh paint and new cloth. She saw a neat array of display cases under shining glass, racks of neatly hung men's suits and women's dresses, hats and button shoes and other accessories—all bearing the price tags of a prosperous boomtown. Looking over this array, Nan Harper thought a little wistfully that with the current state of her grandfather's business, there wasn't a thing here she could afford to buy.

There were few customers at that moment. A male clerk started toward her, but Nan had caught sight of Baby Doe, and she gave the man a smile and shake of the head and moved in her friend's direction. Baby Doe stood leaning against a counter, her golden head bent over a piece of paper she was studying with frowning concentration.

She looked gorgeous, every curl and strand in place. She was dressed simply, in keeping with her occupation, but her features and complexion and the gold brooch at her throat made the shopgirl's costume of shirtwaist and skirt seem somehow a good deal more elegant. When Nan spoke her name, she looked up and smiled a greeting.

Nan asked, "How's the first day going?"

The other woman shrugged. "All right, I suppose. We haven't been very busy so far." She ruefully indicated the paper in her hand. "I think it will take me forever to learn all these prices and where to find all the stock." She tossed the paper aside, as though glad to put it out of her mind.

Nan was looking around at the display of clothing. "It's the first time I've been in. The store looks very nice."

"Jake Sandeloski—Sands, that is—has good taste," Baby Doe agreed. "See anything you like?"

"I see all kinds of things I'd like, but nothing I can afford." Nan added, "I came by to see if you'd be able to go to dinner with me, as we discussed yesterday."

"I think so. Just a minute."

Baby Doe went to speak to the clerk, a mousy-looking fellow whose entire face lighted up eagerly as she approached. They conferred briefly; the man hesitated, then nodded, and was rewarded with a dazzling smile. Baby Doe beckoned to Nan, and when the dark-haired woman joined them, Baby Doe explained, "Harry will cover for me with Jake if I'm not gone too long. Thank you, Harry. You're a prince!" Another smile seemed to make his knees melt. A little enviously, Nan judged that her friend knew exactly what it took to get what she wanted from men.

Moments later they were outside and getting into the buggy. "I thought we'd try the Saddle Rock," Nan suggested. "It's a good restaurant, just up the street."

"You know the town," Baby Doe said. "Whatever you say suits me."

The Saddle Rock was located a short distance north of the Opera House, and on the same side of Harrison Avenue. Entering, they found it well filled. They made their way to a table at the rear, past a barrage of interested male glances aimed at Nan's beautiful companion. Though Baby Doe appeared oblivious to them, Nan didn't think she missed one of the many looks she received; indeed, she seemed to thrive on them.

They took their seats and accepted the menus a waiter offered. Running her eyes over the printed menu, Baby Doe exclaimed, "Fresh oysters! In the middle of the Colorado mountains? My, I'll have to try them!"

"That does sound good," Nan agreed, but she decided upon a chicken stew when she saw the price. They gave their orders, and as they waited the blond woman looked around at the furnishings of the elegant restaurant; in no other of Leadville's eating establishments could brocade draperies and velvet cushions be found. The light from the gas-fueled chandeliers glittered on the crystal goblets and imported silverware. The Saddle Rock drew its share of the better clientele; Nan and Baby Doe could hear considerable angry discussion of the strike, and of the harm it was causing Leadville. There was vague mention of some sort of violence having broken out the night before, and Nan did not hear a single note of sympathy for the miners who had left their jobs in hope of getting decent wages. It bothered her and offended her sense of fair play.

Rather than listen to the talk, she asked Baby Doe, "Well, have you met Horace Tabor yet?"

The blond woman looked at her. "Now how would I be apt to do that?"

"Why, I thought he might have dropped into the store. He owns that building, you know—the Opera House. He has an office and a suite of rooms on the second floor. He stays alone up there."

"Alone? I thought you told me he's married."

"He is. But Augusta—that's his wife—has moved to Denver. Tabor bought them a big house there last fall when he was elected lieutenant governor. But of course his business concerns are all in Leadville, so he has to spend a lot of time here. When he does, he lives upstairs at the Opera House."

Baby Doe nodded indifferently, as though not particularly caring about any of this; but Nan had a feeling she might be more interested than she let on. She let the subject drop. "How did the room work out that I found for you? Are you comfortable there?"

"Oh, it's fine—just fine," Baby Doe said quickly, but her fine blue eyes held an abstract expression.

Their food, when it arrived, was as good as Nan had predicted, and they continued chatting as they ate, but their talk broke off suddenly when someone appeared beside their table. Nan looked up and discovered Morgan Slaughter smiling down at them.

"Nan!" he exclaimed. "And . . . Mrs. Doe, isn't it? What a pleasant surprise to find you both here. I stopped at the stage office," he told Nan. "I asked for you, but your grandfather couldn't tell me where you were. I was disappointed—I barely had a chance to speak to you yesterday when the stage got in."

"I know," she said. And because she sensed he was waiting for an invitation, she suggested, a little reluctantly, "Would you like to join us?"

His hand on the back of a chair, Slaughter hesitated. "If you're sure I won't be intruding. . . ."

He looked boldly at Baby Doe, who gave him an impersonal smile and said, "Not at all." Satisfied, he drew out the chair and took the place facing Nan Harper.

He gestured to a waiter but shook his head when a menu was offered. "I've only got time for a cup of coffee." As the man went off to fetch it, Slaughter explained to Nan, "I've been on the go this morning. I told your grandfather I'd send a crew up to the pass, to clear away that slide—it's up to all of us here in Leadville to keep traffic and supplies moving. Of course, after the railroad comes it'll be someone else's responsibility."

His coffee was brought; he liked it black. As he started

to sip it, Nan asked hesitantly, "Have you heard any more news as to how soon the railroad might be completed?"

"Not really," he told her. "Except that it can only be a matter of weeks, the rate they're laying iron up the valley." Seeing her expression, he added, "That's good news for Leadville, of course; but I'm well aware what it means to you and your grandfather."

"It's our problem. We'll face it when the time comes."

He placed a hand over hers, where it lay on the table. He said quickly, "I've told you before, if you'd only let me—"

"Please!" Nan begged, with a look around her, and slipped her hand free. Morgan Slaughter seemed to remember suddenly where he was, and also to be aware of Baby Doe watching them with a half-amused expression. The blond woman said nothing, but at her look Slaughter flushed a little.

For Nan it had been a painful and awkward moment, especially in so public a place. She didn't know where to look or what to say. It came as a definite relief when she caught sight of a man she knew who had entered the restaurant and was moving directly toward their table.

He was a big man, well dressed but somehow awkward in his carefully tailored clothing. He had a swarthy complexion and was starting to go bald, but what remained of his hair was still black, and so was the full and flowing mustache. From his heavy stride as he bulled his way through the crowded room, heedless of the greetings that were tossed at him from every side, there seemed to be something on Horace Tabor's mind that made him angry; his keen eyes gave his face a hawkish look.

Slaughter seemed unaware of Tabor's presence until the newcomer halted behind his chair and said, in a rough voice, "*Here* you are! Somebody told me they seen you come in. Morgan, I have to talk to you!"

Morgan Slaughter turned and looked up in surprise, then quickly answered, "Sure thing, Horace. I'll be through directly."

"Hurry it up!"

The tall, black-haired man seemed not to have noticed anyone else until Nan Harper said politely, "Good afternoon, Mr. Tabor."

His attention was immediately drawn to her. They had known each other since she was a little girl, and in a pleasanter tone he said, "Why, hello, Nan. How's your grandfather?"

"He's fine," she said. "Would you like to sit down?"

"Can't," he said bluntly. "Little business matter that has to be taken care of. Don't let me interrupt. . . ." But the words seemed to die on his tongue.

Horace Tabor had just seen Baby Doe.

The blond woman hadn't said a word, but Nan sensed that from the moment of realizing this was the man about whom she'd heard so much, Baby Doe had been watching him with the most undisguised interest. Now that his glance had lit on her, Horace Tabor seemed unable to tear his eyes away. In the sudden stillness, Nan proceeded to make the introduction.

"So you're the fabulous Horace Tabor!" Baby Doe exclaimed, with one of her most devastating smiles. She offered her hand across the littered table. "I'm most delighted to meet you."

As though struck dumb, Tabor accepted the hand. He held it longer than was strictly necessary, and let it go only with reluctance. Then, seeming to forget everything he had been saying a moment earlier, he proceeded to pull out the remaining chair and lower himself into it, moving like someone in a trance.

The waiter came rushing up to greet him and thrust a menu into his hands, anxious to be of service. "And your pleasure today, Mr. Tabor?"

Horace Tabor looked blankly at him and at the piece of cardboard. He shook himself together. "Come to think of it," he said, "for a fact, I ain't eaten yet. You can bring me a steak—rare. And the trimmin's."

"Yes, Mr. Tabor," the waiter exclaimed, bobbing his

head. "The chef knows just the way you like it. It'll be coming right up!" He rushed off.

Tabor was once more staring at the woman seated across from him. He started to speak, cleared his throat, and tried again. "Don't reckon I've seen you around, Mrs. Doe. If I had, I sure as hell would have remembered."

She smiled, showing him her dimples. "I'm new in your city, Mr. Tabor. I came from Denver—arrived on the stage just yesterday."

As he got control of himself, Horace Tabor became more effusive. "Well now, I'm sure that's a right nice break for Leadville! I hope everybody's treatin' you the way they should."

"I couldn't possibly complain," Baby Doe assured him. "But thank you."

Nan was growing increasingly uncomfortable. She was well aware that this restaurant table, with the golden-haired stranger and the richest man in Leadville, had become the open target of every eye in the place. However, she saw something happening here that disturbed her even more than that. She couldn't resist asking the big man beside her, "How is Mrs. Tabor?"

"What?" The swarthy features darkened as the question registered. If he felt some irritation at her pointed reminder, he made an effort to conceal it. "Got a letter from her, just last week," he said. "Augusta's fine. Why shouldn't she be, with that big house I bought her in Denver?"

Which the poor woman probably hates! Nan thought silently. A person of simple tastes and expectations, Augusta Tabor had been happy for all those long years of working together with her husband to scrape a meager living out of the Colorado wilderness. Nan was sure their sudden affluence made Augusta miserable. The mansion in Denver could be no substitute for the plain clapboard house that had once been their Leadville home, humble but happy.

Nan Harper sighed and shook her head at the strange quirks and ironies of fate.

Tabor was chatting again with Baby Doe; he seemed to be trying to learn all he could about her. "Your husband's here too, Mrs. Doe?"

"I have no husband," she said matter-of-factly.

He managed a look of sympathetic alarm. "A *widow*?" he exclaimed. "And so young! Ma'am, I'm right sorry to hear that."

She met his look squarely. "Not a widow, Mr. Tabor. I'm divorced."

"Oh." He seemed to take that in stride. "Any children?" When she shook her head, Tabor smoothed his flowing mustache with the palm of a hand and told her, "Well, I hope you'll find things ripe for a better beginnin', here in Leadville."

"Thank you," she said earnestly. "Actually, I feel very sure of it."

Morgan Slaughter's coffee cup chimed against its saucer as he drained it and set it down. "I'm finished, Horace. Ready to hear whatever it is you wanted to take up with me."

Tabor gave him a frown as though he'd forgotten the matter. He said impatiently, "Looks like it'll have to wait. I got a steak comin', and besides, this is no place to talk business. Could you be at my office—say an hour from now?"

"I'll try to make it." Slaughter got to his feet.

Horace Tabor looked up at him, and there was a return of his initial coldness upon entering the restaurant. "You do that," he suggested shortly. "Try real hard!"

Nan Harper pushed her own chair back as she looked at Baby Doe. "Isn't it time we were getting back to work, too?" she suggested.

"Hey, now!" Horace Tabor exclaimed quickly. "You aren't all goin' to rush off and leave me?" He appealed to the blond woman across the table from him. "*You'll* stay just a little while, won't you? I want a chance to get better acquainted."

Plainly, he was anxious not to let her get away. As for Baby Doe, if she remembered her solemn promise made to the clerk who was covering her absence on this first day on a new job, she didn't let it bother her. She tossed her golden head as she answered lightly, "Of course. Why not?" And she settled comfortably in her chair.

Just a little put out with her, Nan rose, saying, "Well *my* job won't wait."

"I'll escort you," Morgan Slaughter offered quickly, and she nodded since she could think of no good reason to refuse.

"Sure," Horace Tabor said gruffly, with a wave of the hand. "You two run along. Don't worry about the bill—I'm takin' care of it."

There was a trace of stiffness in her manner as Nan thanked him. Without another word for Baby Doe, she let Slaughter take her arm and escort her out of the Saddle Rock to the place where her buggy waited.

He helped her in and then climbed up beside her. As he took the reins, he commented dryly, "I would say your friend has made a conquest! She's a damned attractive woman; I can't deny her that. But—does she understand that Tabor has a family?"

Nan felt no desire at all to discuss the subject with him. She said briskly, "It was mentioned."

"I'm glad to hear that! At least, then, she knows the situation. As for Tabor—well, I suppose he's at an age when a man feels like kicking over the traces. Augusta's kept him on a pretty tight leash all these years. Now with her in Denver and Horace on his own . . ." He broke off. "Well, I shouldn't criticize."

Nan was relieved when he gave the bay a slap with the reins, as though dropping the matter, and eased them out into the traffic along Harrison Avenue. But Morgan Slaughter had more to say. "Nan," he said in an earnest tone, "I don't pretend to be perfect, but there's one thing

I feel strongly about—the marriage institution. Lord knows I'm no holier than most bachelors, but I figure marriage isn't to be taken lightly, the way some men seem able to do. One of these days, once this damnable strike is settled and out of the way, I don't think it comes as any great surprise that I'm going to have something I'll want to ask you. . . ."

She sat quiet on the seat next to him, her cold fingers tightly clenched, caught up in a storm of embarrassment. Surely, she thought in her misery, someone like Baby Doe must have had plenty of experience in handling an unwanted suitor; she probably could have told her exactly what to say and do. But this was a predicament Nan had never imagined happening to her, plain as she considered herself to be. She bit her lip, wishing desperately that Morgan Slaughter had never spoken those words and utterly at a loss as to how to respond to them.

Then something happened, and she didn't have to.

With a sudden exclamation, Morgan Slaughter hauled in on the reins; the buggy stopped with a lurch. The bay horse tossed up its head in protest, and Nan caught the grab iron to steady herself. Without warning, three men had stepped out into the traffic, evidently meaning to cross to the avenue's west side. Two of them were holding the third by the arms, as he marched between them. Now almost directly in the path of the buggy, the prisoner made an attempt to break free. He jerked loose, and the next instant a blow was struck that sent him to his knees.

"What in the world!" Nan exclaimed in horror. "What do those men think they're doing?"

"Damned if I know." Slaughter spoke curtly, busy controlling the startled horse. All around them traffic was halting, held up by the disturbance in the middle of the street. Now the prisoner was being yanked unceremoniously to his feet, and Nan had a better look at all three men. She saw the gleam of sunlight on a gun barrel, and she saw the face of the one who held it. She recognized him. Her hand closed on Slaughter's arm, feeling the hard muscle through his coat sleeve. She exclaimed, "Isn't that your man—Tom Riordan?"

Her companion turned his head and looked at her directly for the briefest of moments—but long enough for her to see the coldness in his stare and the ironlike set of his face. This time he said nothing at all but turned abruptly away again; a newcomer had stepped out into the dust of the street. Nan's eyes widened she saw it was Griff Cameron. He, too, had a gun in his hand, and he called out sharply in a tone that carried above all other sounds: "Let go of him. *Now!*"

Slaughter's man swung about to stare at him; she saw the look on Riordan's face. Nan caught her breath in the virtual certainty that she was about to see gunplay—perhaps a killing—right there in front of her.

Chapter Seven

Griff Cameron was hardly aware of anything except for the trio of men who stood watching him approach. That others might be watching—that all traffic around them had stalled, with horsedrawn rigs halted in the middle of the thoroughfare—scarcely registered with him at all. His whole attention was narrowed on Mike Malloy, looking dazed from the fist that had smeared the lower part of his face with blood, and on the pair who held him prisoner. This sight excluded everything else, just as the brim of Griff's hat cut away the brilliant glare of midday sunlight pouring down on him from overhead.

The man who had been pointed out to him as Tom Riordan spoke, his voice as challenging as the hard stab of his eyes. "Whoever you are, this has got nothing to do with you that I know of, mister. You'd better back off!"

"I'm afraid not," Griff retorted. "The man happens to be a friend of mine."

"Then maybe you know that he's been ordered out of this town. He had the chance to leave, but he wouldn't take it. Now we're seeing to it that he goes!"

Looking past Riordan, Griff saw that, in fact, everything had been arranged for Malloy's departure. Yonder on the far side of the avenue a man was holding saddled horses in readiness, for Mike Malloy and his captors to mount and leave Leadville. *To be seen no more*—Griff remembered the ominous wording of the note. At the thought his jaw hardened, and his fingers tightened on the revolver. Just then the man with the horses lifted his head; sunlight struck the fellow's face, and Griff saw the sheen of reddish whiskers—and with a start he knew he was looking at Ed Luft!

Luft returned his stare, across half the width of Harrison Avenue, and Griff had an uncanny feeling that the other man knew him and knew precisely what had brought him to Leadville. There was one moment of mutual recognition; then Griff had to pull his attention back to the scene before him, for there had been a sudden interruption.

From the crowd that had gathered along the edge of the street, a man suddenly pushed forward calling Riordan's name. Griff Cameron turned quickly and saw the miner, Frank Gower, his broken left arm in its sling—and in the other hand, a rifle, which he held with its butt clamped beneath his elbow. Gower called out, "We know how you mean to handle this, Riordan! Once you've ridden him out of town, that'll be the end of him!" He brandished the rifle. "Maybe you'd like to find out how well I can manage this thing one handed?"

All at once the odds had been evened, two against two. Tom Riordan's head had sunk forward a little, his stocky shape taking on the stance of a man squaring himself for battle. Mike Malloy, pressing the back of a hand to his bleeding face, shook his head in a mute plea with his friends not to let gunplay develop on his account.

In that tense moment Griff Cameron sensed that a gesture, a single word, was all it would take. There was the sound of boots shuffling on sidewalk plankings as onlookers began to move out of range of wild bullets.

The break came from an unexpected quarter. Griff was aware that vehicles had come to a standstill, blocked by this disturbance, but he had been able to give them little attention. Now he heard a voice and recognized it as

Nan's. His head jerked around, and he saw her on the seat of a buggy that was halted so close to him that he could have reached out and touched the bay horse standing uneasily between its shafts. She was clutching the arm of Morgan Slaughter, who held the reins beside her, and her face was drained white as she exclaimed, "You have to stop this, Morgan! Please! You *have* to!"

Slaughter sat like a rock, his expression unyielding, but something in her words must have had their effect. Scowling and with evident reluctance, he shrugged and shoved the reins at Nan. As she took them, he slid across the seat, and the rig settled under his weight as he heaved himself out and stepped down into the dust.

He walked forward to join the group who confronted one another in the center of the street. His cold stare rested briefly on Griff Cameron, passed over the bleeding Malloy, and finally settled on his own man, Tom Riordan. He demanded heavily, "All right! What appears to be the trouble?"

Riordan made a brief gesture. "Nothing I can't handle." He would have turned away, but the tone of Slaughter's next words pulled him back.

"I asked you a question!" Morgan Slaughter reminded him flatly. "I expect an answer." He indicated the bleeding face of the Irishman, Mike Malloy. "What are you doing to this man?"

Watching, Griff saw a strange medley of expressions pass over Tom Riordan's face as his boss's voice hit him: anger, and something like bewildered disbelief, as though this rebuke was the last thing he had expected. To feel the rough edge of Slaughter's tongue must have taken him totally unaware, and he seemed for the moment unable to speak.

Griff suggested, "Mike, where's the letter? Why don't we see what Mr. Slaughter here has to say about that."

Malloy hesitated and then without a word got it from his pocket. When he held it out, Morgan Slaughter seemed

reluctant to accept it. Griff watched as the mineowner
unfolded the crumpled piece of paper and scowled at its
contents. Somehow Griff was convinced he only pretended
to read the words—that he was actually stalling while he
made up his mind how to deal with this. Griff jogged him
with a question.

"Does it look familiar?" he demanded. "I understand
Malloy's not the first man this Committee of One Hundred has ordered out of Leadville. He's just the first who
refused to go. We've been waiting to see what would
happen, and your boy Riordan has just been showing us."

Both men gave Griff a furious stare, then Slaughter
looked at Nan, who was observing all this from the seat of
the buggy. She seemed to make up his mind for him.
Shrugging, he deliberately tore the letter to shreds and
then dropped them into the street dust.

"I knew nothing at all about it," he said—for the
woman's benefit, Griff was sure. "If this sort of thing has
been going on, it was kept a secret from me—for reasons
obvious to anyone that knows me! I would never have
gone along with such a business, nor can I allow anyone
who works for me to have any part in it." He turned to
Riordan then. "Is that clear?"

Under the corrosive weight of Slaughter's stare, a tide
of color flowed into the man's face. He began to stammer.
"Hell! I only done what I figured you—"

Slaughter's arm swept around and the flat of his palm
struck Riordan, with a slap that sounded sharply in the
listening quiet. The print of fingers contrasting against the
angry blood-red flush of his cheeks, Riordan's shoulders
lifted, and for an instant he seemed ready to lunge at his
employer. A breath swelled his chest, and he stared blankly
at Slaughter as the mineowner thundered, "Don't put
your stupidity onto *me*!"

Slaughter stabbed a finger at Mike Malloy. "This
man," he went on, his eyes probing Riordan's, "has been a
nuisance and a troublemaker! He's done more than any-

one else to keep the strike going and cripple the mining industry and Leadville itself. But it's still a free country. Long as he stays within the law, he's not to be touched. I hope that's clear enough for even you to understand!"

Before his challenging stare, Tom Riordan wavered and gave way. The man gave a shrug and answered sullenly, "You're the boss."

"Try not to forget it! I'll talk to you later," the mineowner added, and cuffed him slightly on the shoulder. "Let's move on, now. We've made a spectacle of ourselves and held up traffic long enough!"

With that Slaughter turned his back on the man. For just an instant his glance fell on Griff Cameron and held there, in frowning speculation. Abruptly he swung away and returned to the buggy, where Nan Harper had sat watching. He climbed in and, without speaking, took the reins from her and slapped the bay horse on the rump. She seemed very grave and was silent as they continued up the street, passing close to the spot where Griff Cameron stood and watched them go by.

When she had first seen Slaughter's hired man participating in the struggle on the street, she had thought the mineowner was responsible, and his hesitation to get involved fueled that assumption. But once he had jumped down from the buggy to put an end to the confrontation, Nan gained a new measure of respect for Morgan Slaughter, dismissing as foolishness any notions of his involvement.

The scene there in the street broke up then, and traffic resumed. Tom Riordan, after a last scowling glare at Griff, turned around and strode away, his partner beside him. Griff, still staring after Riordan, heard Mike Malloy saying something and felt the Irishman's hand on his sleeve, trying to draw his attention.

But suddenly Griff Cameron had only one thing in mind. Ignoring the traffic beginning to flow around him, he was searching the crowd for Ed Luft—but the red-bearded man was gone.

Instantly Griff started off at a run, dodging a freight wagon and nearly colliding with a swerving horseman. Luft had been holding four saddled mounts; now one was missing. A searching glance in both directions along Harrison Avenue showed no sign of his man. Griff caught up the reins of one of the remaining animals, found the stirrup, and swung hurriedly astride.

If Luft was running, there was only one route he could have taken. Griff rode to the first cross street, hoping to see the man on the long block sloping westward, downhill from Harrison Avenue; but Ed Luft had a bigger lead than that. Nor was there any sight of him to right or left when Griff reached the next corner. Disappointed, he curbed his horse while he hunted for prints, not able to tell much from the rutted street surface.

The horse describing a nervous circle under him, Griff Cameron swore. Finally he thought he could just make out a faint cloud of dust hanging in the air where the hooves of another mount had placed it. Gambling, he reined his animal hard left.

A sudden gust of wind flung up grit, making him duck his head and scattering any trace of dust there might have been. He kept on doggedly, but with ebbing confidence that he would find Ed Luft. It was maddening to have had the man he was searching for in view, then lose him again—all in a matter of minutes. After riding another half block; he again hauled on the reins, ready to turn back and try a different route. But in that moment of uncertainty, he distinctly heard the whiffling snort from the nostrils of a horse, very near at hand.

A high wooden fence with a gate rose beside him. On an impulse Griff slid from the saddle, his gun ready as he approached the gate. It was unfastened, hanging slightly ajar. He heard a shod hoof strike the fence, hard. Cautiously he pushed the gate open.

He found himself looking into someone's backyard, perhaps fenced off to hold a vicious dog or to protect an attempt at a garden. Just now it was littered with trash but otherwise empty—except for the horse standing under saddle and on trailing reins. Griff couldn't swear from looking at the animal that it was one of the four Luft had been holding, but its state of excitement gave it away; it stomped, tossed its head, and flashed its eyes in a way that told it had been running hard and was a long way from settling down.

Then a sound brought Griff's head sharply to his left. Another gate at the front of the lot was closing, with a faint creak and a thud as it swung to. Griff headed for it, avoiding the litter of rusting cans and broken bottles, and jerked the gate open.

He was expecting a gunshot, but it failed to come. His own weapon drawn, he eased through the gate to a weedy path that led to the next street. Briefly, he thought he heard the scuff of running footsteps; that was enough to send him hurrying ahead. He broke into the open and peered hastily around, but found the street deserted. Even when he ran along the row of buildings, searching the spaces between, he saw no sign of anyone. After a few more steps, he gave it up.

It was plain enough—his man had eluded him again. Ed Luft could be hiding, ready to put a bullet in him if he came blundering too close. More likely, he was putting distance between them while Griff stood here uselessly debating.

He swore softly and lowered the gun, realizing he had once more drawn a blank—just when he had seemed on the verge of success.

Griff Cameron's thoughts were bleak as he rode back into town, trailing the horse that he had rescued from the yard where Luft had abandoned it. During his abortive chase, Harrison Avenue had returned again to normal, almost as though no confrontation had taken place in the middle of the street. The extra pair of saddled horses still stood at a hitching rack; Griff dismounted and left the other two with them, for someone else to claim and tend to.

He noticed Mike Malloy and Frank Gower standing on the opposite walk, in serious conversation with a third man he didn't know. When they saw him approaching, they broke off, turning, and as they did, sunlight reflected off something metal pinned to the coat of the stranger.

A *badge!* Griff gave a start and nearly faltered, but it was too late to turn back. He steeled himself not to betray any of the alarm he felt as he stepped up onto the plank sidewalk.

Malloy spoke. "This is Jud Osland," he said, indicating the man with the badge. "He's town marshal here. He'd like to talk to you."

Griff looked at the officer and waited. The man's intelligent eyes, set in a homely face beneath a mop of grizzled hair, regarded him narrowly. "They tell me your name's Cameron," the marshal finally said.

"That's right."

Gesturing toward Malloy and Gower, the marshal said, "The boys here have been telling me about that business in the street. Seems I arrived too late to do anything about it. I'll be checking with some other people, later. Right now you're the one that interests me. You're a newcomer to Leadville?"

Griff nodded with apprehension, afraid that the detective for the stage company he had worked for had found him—and just when he was so close to nailing the real culprit!

"A complete outsider—and yet from what I hear, you stepped into something that was none of your concern. You make a practice of that?"

"Only when I don't like the odds," Griff answered shortly. "Or when I don't like the shape of what's happening. I'd met these two last evening and heard something about their problem. From what I've seen in the short time I've been here, looks to me they're in the right."

Not having solicited Griff's opinion on the strike, Marshal Osland didn't pick up on it or give any sign of his own attitude, if he had one. Instead he remarked, "As I was walking up I saw you run across the street, jump into the saddle, and take off like somebody was after you—or maybe the other way around. I'm a little curious."

Griff shrugged. "I thought I spotted someone I've been trying to see. If it was him, I missed him."

"Would he be the reason you came to Leadville?"

"Could be."

The lawman's stare continued to rest on him, as if challenging the scanty answers he was getting. Griff made himself meet the look, and after a moment Osland turned to Malloy.

"I keep getting reports of a near riot last night on Fryer Hill. No one hurt bad—some heads busted, and maybe a bone or two." He looked pointedly at Frank Gower with his conspicuously bandaged arm. But Gower just looked back, and the marshal's features darkened. "It seems damned strange!" he went on, his voice roughening. "So far I can't seem to find anyone who'll even admit he was there, or is willing to come forward and file a complaint so I can try to arrest somebody. How do they expect the law to function?"

Malloy said bluntly, "The only thing we want is our rights, Marshal, and we'll fight for them if we have to. We don't ask the law, or anybody else, to do our fighting."

The lawman's scowl deepened. "It's my job to keep order in this town. And by God, I'll bust any man I catch making that job any harder!" Abruptly he turned on his heel and stalked away.

Griff felt some of his tension slip away. "That's a tough man to figure," he remarked gruffly. "Is he for you or against you?"

Frank Gower gave a snort. He spoke from bitter

disillusionment. "Hell, the whole city government belongs to Tabor and the rest of the owners. Figure it out for yourself."

But Malloy, with a troubled shake of the head, said slowly, "I think Jud Osland means just what he says. I take him for an honest man. He's caught in the middle by this strike, and he's under a lot of pressure."

The Irishman's cheek was still bleeding. Watching him stanch it with a handkerchief, Griff asked anxiously, "Are you all right?"

"Sure." Malloy shrugged. "Disgusted with myself, mostly—to think I could let 'em take me that easy! Hell, I thought I was on my guard! But Riordan and that other one was waiting for me. First I knew, they closed in, punched me in the face, and had a gun in my ribs. I'm lucky to still be alive!"

"Maybe you've learned now that you can't be too careful," Gower said darkly. "Since you defied that letter, you can bet they're going to be trying for you again."

Griff had a different idea. "I'm not so sure about that," he told Malloy. "You called their bluff. Slaughter's had to make a public statement, in front of the town, that nothing more will happen to you. For the time being, at least, he's going to have to call his men off and see they keep that promise."

Gower gave a snort of disbelief, but Malloy appeared thoughtful. Now he remembered something else. "The man that you went after just now. That was Ed Luft?"

Griff nodded. "He was in with Riordan, tending the horses that were supposed to take the lot of you out of town, where they could have done to you whatever it was they had in mind. But he knew I'd seen him, and he took off. He disappeared on me."

"Well, by God, maybe we can help!" Frank Gower exclaimed. "Let me round up a bunch of the boys. Show us where it was you lost him, and we'll run the bastard to earth."

"Too late, I'm afraid. He's had plenty of time to put himself out of reach. Holed up somewhere, or more likely cleared out. We'd never find him now."

"You're probably right," Malloy said regretfully. "I wish we *could* help. I really owe you—I was close to a goner till you stepped in."

"I'm not really the one you have to thank," Griff said.

"Who, then?" Gower retorted. "We sure as hell ain't gonna believe Slaughter called his wolves off out of the goodness of his heart."

Griff looked at him. "You really don't know what happened? Why, it was Nan Harper! She shamed him into calling a halt to it. You've all got reason to be grateful to her," he said earnestly. "She's someone pretty special."

"You think so?" Gower looked dubious. "If she's so special, why does she have anything to do with a bastard like Slaughter? The whole town knows the play he's making for her—and I ain't aware that she's made any effort to turn him off."

Griff Cameron was startled at his own reaction, at the sudden burst of anger that made him turn on the other man. When he spoke, his voice was quiet, but there was a livid edge to it. "Careful! If I were you I wouldn't say anything I wasn't ready to prove."

Gower blinked and backed off a step. When Mike Malloy spoke, there was a look of understanding on his honest Irish face. "I think we're all worked up to where we may say things we don't mean. Personally, I could use a drop of the old stuff about now. Just one—then I better be getting home. My Mary could be wondering what's been going on. What do you say? Will you lads join me?"

Griff Cameron looked at Gower and nodded. "It's fine with me."

"Yeah, me too." Gower looked a trifle shamefaced. "If I spoke out of turn," he added gruffly, "I didn't mean nothing."

Griff nodded his acceptance of the apology; what bothered him most were the unexpected feelings brought explosively to light by an offhand remark concerning a woman he scarcely knew. . . .

Neither Nan Harper nor Morgan Slaughter spoke as they rode the remaining distance to the stage yard after the fracas in the street broke up. After they came in through the gate, he brought the rig to a halt and sat, silently, the reins in his hands. Nan looked at him, wondering at his thoughts and waiting for what he might have to say about the scene she had witnessed.

Finally, stirring his solid bulk, he spoke gruffly. "Sorry you had to watch that. On the other hand, it's good that we were there, so I could stop it from going too far."

She paused for a moment, then said quietly, "Hadn't it already gone too far?"

He gave her a sidelong look, but then he sighed and nodded. "Of course, you're right. I'm just going to have to make clear to Tom Riordan and the rest of my men that I won't allow such things."

"What was in the letter you tore up?"

"Foolishness." He shrugged. "Not worth discussing. It's this damnable strike!" he went on, his voice growing hot. "The longer it drags out, the more it causes people to do and say things they normally wouldn't. People on both sides!"

Nan said, with feeling, "It frightens me to think what could still happen. Somebody may end up getting killed." She hesitated, knowing what she had to say even if it proved a waste of breath and effort. "Wouldn't it be better to try coming to terms? Three dollars seems mighty little for a whole day's wages."

She saw how his head went up, how he stiffened in resistance at the suggestion. "Nan, you don't understand these things. It's entirely out of the question!"

"But those men work so *hard*!"

"If we let them win on this," he retorted, adamant, "there's no saying what they'll be demanding next. Before you know, they'll be telling me and Horace Tabor and the other owners how we're to run our business. And we can't allow that!" He dismissed the matter, saying, "Right now I think I'd better be finding out what Tabor wanted to see me about."

He climbed from the buggy and came around to help her down. But when Nan gave him her hand, he paused, peering up at her with a frowning expression. Without warning he asked, "That fellow Cameron—just what do you know about him, anyway?"

Puzzled, she answered, "Not terribly much. Just that he's had experience with stagecoaching. You were there when he turned down the job Grandpa offered him."

"You've got no hint as to why he's here in Leadville?"

"Not really." She added, "Of course, I haven't any intention of prying."

"Well, I don't know." Slaughter was plainly dissatisfied. "There's something damned funny going on. He arrives here yesterday, from nowhere. And today he pushes his way into an argument he had no business interfering with. I'd just like to know what he's up to."

Nan heard herself retorting, "He said he didn't like what he saw. And I feel exactly the same!"

"Oh?" His frown deepened. "So now you're standing up for him?" He seemed to want to say more, but he bit it off. He shrugged and stepped back, and with little ceremony helped her to the ground. But as he did she saw the look on his face, and she wondered suddenly, *Does he think I'm interested in Griff Cameron?*

The thought of anyone being jealous over her was so unfamiliar that she quickly dismissed it. But later, thinking of that scene, Nan wondered if it might actually be true. She wasn't sure she liked the idea, though it might be different if she felt something for Morgan Slaughter. But she didn't; and she had never done more than try to be pleasant to him, because she felt it could be beneficial to her grandfather. Actually, she had come, in time, to resent Slaughter's almost possessive attitude.

But then came an alarming thought: Morgan Slaughter was not one to let another man stand in his way—in anything. What if she had become an innocent source of danger for Griff Cameron, a danger he would never even be aware of? At the thought, the breath caught in her throat.

Chapter Eight

Horace Tabor had never known an hour to pass so swiftly or so pleasantly. He was surprised at himself. He considered himself a mature man of the world, with his fiftieth birthday staring him in the face, and here he was smitten like a schoolboy. Since wealth had begun to pour in on him—and especially during the past six months that Augusta had been safely ensconced in the mansion in Denver—there had been quite a procession of women through his bachelor quarters on the second floor of the Opera House. But the one across the table from him in the Saddle Rock was something totally new to his experience.

In the presence of so much youth and golden beauty, to say nothing of her incredible blue eyes, in which he thought he might drown, Tabor was aware of a change coming over him. A weight of bitterness and disappointment, the residue of near-poverty and drudgery, of fruitless dreams . . . all that seemed now to slip away from him. Basking in Baby Doe's admiring attention, he was young again. His fumbling speech became almost eloquent; he talked about himself, and she listened, intent on each word he uttered.

He learned as much as he needed to know for now

about this wonderful woman—that she was recently divorced, unattached, alone here in Leadville, and employed in a clothing establishment on the lower floor of his own building. When she suddenly rose and exclaimed in alarm that her lunch break had lasted far too long, Tabor pulled out a massive silver watch, snapped open the case, and blinked in astonishment as he saw the time.

"I had no idea we'd been sittin' here this long!" he said as he rose and shoved back his chair. "I got work waitin' myself. Since we're obviously goin' in the same direction, I'll be more'n pleased if you let me escort you."

She accepted warmly. Tabor summoned the bill for the whole table, tossed out a handful of silver dollars in payment, and gave Baby Doe his arm as they left the restaurant. Moving along the sidewalk with this fascinating creature beside him, he knew that the envious looks he encountered were for something other than his wealth and power. The realization put a spring into his step; the weight of nearly fifty years fell away, and with it the fumbling awkwardness of his outsized frame. He felt like a young and handsome man.

He saw her to the door of her place of employment, taking off his hat as he told her, "If Jake Sands gives you any trouble because of bein' late, you tell him it was all my fault. Just send him to me and I'll settle his feathers. After all, I'm his landlord."

When Baby Doe laughed, her head tilted back and her voice sounded golden; he admired the line of her perfect throat. Letting her hand rest a moment longer on his sleeve, she said, "I'm not much afraid of Jake. And I've had a most wonderful time. Any woman would be proud to dine with the fabulous Horace Tabor!"

"Oh, come now!" he protested, without much conviction. After a pause, he took her hand and said, "You enjoy goin' to the theater?"

"Oh, I love it!"

"We got a new bill openin' tonight. I'd be proud to

have you as my guest—I have a private box—that is, if you'd be interested."

She would indeed. He made arrangements for his carriage to pick her up at her rooming house, and promised a supper that would satisfy royalty after the evening's performance. Again she laughed gaily, turning toward the door, and he watched her vanish into the store, chuckling a little to himself.

In the lobby of the Opera House, he walked past a display of posters for the current attraction, past the closed ticket window, and up the wide stairway. A set of double doors on the landing led into the auditorium, and he stepped through them for a moment before going on to his private quarters.

Of all his accomplishments, Horace Tabor was proudest of his Opera House—more than his silver mines, his bank, his hotel, more than his newspaper and his illuminating-gas company, which had changed the very look of Leadville. He stood now with the auditorium sweeping away before him to the dress circle and orchestra pit. The cast-iron seats were the best available, each one painted gold and upholstered in scarlet plush. The frescoed ceiling, the carpeted aisles, the boxes on either side of the stage, paneled with mirrors and hung with the most costly of handmade curtains . . . all of it combined to create what the newspapers called the largest and best showcase west of the Mississippi. In Tabor's eyes it was a jewel box. Everyone agreed it had changed Leadville from a raw mining camp into a real city.

Down on the stage the curtain was up and the footlights burning, and the touring company scheduled to open a week's run that evening began a rehearsal, familiarizing themselves with the theater. But Horace Tabor scarcely noticed them or heard their voices echoing through the empty hall. He was strangely distracted from the beauty of his creation; another vision hung like a mist before his eyes—the golden-haired beauty of the young Baby Doe.

Tabor ran a palm over the fall of his luxuriant mustache, letting the image of her fill his thoughts—a picture of her seated beside him in his private box. Turning away then, he left the auditorium and climbed the steps to the next floor, where his suite was located.

His mood was broken the moment he crossed the threshold and saw Morgan Slaughter.

Slaughter was standing at Tabor's curved walnut desk; he had just helped himself to a cigar from a silver box and was in the act of biting off the end. Tabor grunted, "Oh. It's you."

Slaughter used the spittoon beside the desk. "I've been waiting. You said you wanted to see me."

Tabor nodded, as though he only now remembered. He closed the door and came into the room. It was immense, with two high windows overlooking Harrison Avenue, and a door leading to the rest of the suite. This was his office, and he had spent money here, as he did on everything. The floor was thickly carpeted, the furnishings rich and ornate; the curtains at the windows fell in heavy folds. A bear's head hung on one wall, the rack of a moose on another. Elaborate gas fixtures, among the first to be installed in Leadville, hung from the ceiling.

Slaughter dropped into one of the big leather chairs and hitched a leg comfortably across its arm, then proceeded to get his cigar burning.

Tabor tossed his hat on the desk and looked at the other man, scowling. He said gruffly, "I was sort of held up."

Slaughter blew a cloud of smoke and flipped his dead match at the spittoon. "I noticed," he said. He took the cigar from his mouth and examined the burning end. "I glanced into the Saddle Rock as I came by. You and the delectable Mrs. Doe looked like you were prepared to spend the afternoon. Quite an eyeful, isn't she?"

Tabor's scowl deepened. Leave it to this man, he thought sourly, to cheapen the rare emotions he had been feeling—to remind him that he was just another middle-aged, married man attracted by a pretty young face.

He went around the desk, lowered himself into his leather-padded chair, and stared for a moment at Morgan Slaughter, Tabor's blunt fingers drumming the polished wood of the desktop. When he had his temper under control, he said, "I called you up here because we got somethin' we need to discuss."

"All right." Slaughter leaned his head back and blew a smoke ring toward the room's high ceiling. "Shoot."

"I want to know what happened last night up on Fryer Hill. If what I heard was true, I don't think I like it."

Slaughter shrugged. "That doesn't tell me much," he pointed out easily. "How do I know what you heard?"

"I heard some of them strikers was holdin' a peaceable meetin', and in the middle of it a bunch of armed toughs jumped in and beat some of them up. What's more, the report I got had your man, Riordan, in charge of the attackers. Now . . . is any part of that true?"

"Of course," Slaughter replied without hesitation, swinging his feet to the floor. "All of it. Tom did a good job. It was time somebody showed those bastards we aren't going to put up with their nonsense forever."

Tabor stiffened angrily. "I take it those were the men you talked me into puttin' out money to hire, to protect our property, you said. But I don't remember bein' told they'd be sent to bust heads! And while we're on the subject—I seem to have been hearin', too, about people bein' threatened and chased out of town. I don't see the need for *that* kind of thing, either."

"Maybe you want to sit back and turn everything over to these strikers."

"Hell, no! But I'm against threats and busted heads," Tabor insisted. "Malloy and the others promised us, right from the beginnin', they wouldn't be usin' violence. So far they never have. Why do we have to be the ones to start it?"

Slaughter considered him through a film of cigar smoke. "You know, if that railroad would just get finished," he suggested coolly, "the problem would solve itself. Cheap labor would be pouring in here. This strike would be over in no time—and we could pay any wage we happened to feel like paying. Maybe you can afford to wait," he went on, "but the rest of us don't have your resources. Far as I'm concerned, every day that silver ore lies useless in the ground is simply one more day without income. And there's another thing I should think even you'd be concerned about."

Tabor's stubby fingers again drummed the desk. "And that is?"

"You must know that with the pumps closed down, some of the mines are already starting to flood out in the lower levels. If that goes on too long, we'll never be able to bring them back. I tell you, for that reason if no other, we've *got* to do something—and soon—to end this damned strike! There isn't any choice."

Deeply troubled, Horace Tabor swung to his feet and strode over to the window, where he could stare down into the dusty street. He didn't see the other man's speculative and measuring look. "Of course," Slaughter remarked, "if you object so much to the kind of men I've been hiring, maybe we have something we could use instead."

Tabor turned from the window. "Oh? What?"

"The Tabor Guard."

He blinked. "Hell! That's nothing but a marchin' society I put together, so the fellows could have some fun!"

"I know. But think about it," Slaughter went on patiently. "The guard has organization . . . officers . . . discipline. What's more, they look damned impressive in those uniforms you outfitted them with. Only one thing you didn't provide for them: guns."

Horace Tabor stared in astonishment.

"So, Horace, I had an idea. Governor Pitkin knows

our problem here. It being an election year, he won't want things to get completely out of hand. And I'm sure he'd rather not have to declare martial law here, for the same reason. But supposing, now, you were to get a wire off to Denver, and tell Pitkin your guard has got to have arms to keep order in this town—or else he can call in the militia. Coming from his own lieutenant governor, I'll wager he can't do less than oblige."

Tabor was vigorously shaking his head. "No. I don't like it at all. Things just ain't got to that state, Morgan."

"You think not?" Slaughter, eyes narrowed, head tilted to one side, studied him. "You may think differently when I tell you something I've been hearing. Those bastards leading the strike think they have a way to teach you a lesson you'll never forget."

"How?"

Slaughter gestured with the hand that held the cigar. "By setting a torch to this building," he said.

The words rocked Tabor's head upon his shoulders, and the blood drained from his cheeks. He looked about him at the elegantly furnished office. He could almost smell the smoke, see the flames sweeping through his beloved theater. . . . He cried hoarsely, "They . . . they wouldn't dare!"

Morgan Slaughter shrugged as he got to his feet. "Suit yourself. I did what I could. I warned you." He started for the door.

He was halfway across the big room when a muffled exclamation halted him and turned him back. Tabor's fists were clenched, his breathing shallow. "I've tried to play fair." His voice was gravelly with emotion. "But if that's the way they want it, all right! I'll get a wire off to the governor. Today! You'll have your guns!"

"Good." Slaughter showed his teeth in a grin of approval. "We'll show those sons of bitches what the score is!"

*　　*　　*

The day had proven to be a tense and aggravating one for Griff Cameron. By intervening in the confrontation with Tom Riordan, in full view of Harrison Avenue, he had drawn the eyes of Leadville to himself. Now, wherever he went in this town, he was aware of the stares that followed him—some merely cautious, others showing unveiled hostility. One thing was certain: He'd made an enemy in Riordan, to say nothing of Riordan's boss. And he was sure he had not heard the last of it.

But what most concerned him was that, for the second time since coming to Leadville, Ed Luft had been almost in his hand and had eluded him. This time, the ground seemed to have swallowed the bearded man up. Griff was left with a keen sense of time passing—and of nothing to show for it.

He could do no more than doggedly continue the search and keep his eyes open. He had been putting out feelers, asking questions, but in answer he drew shrugs or hostile stares or, at best, a sympathetic shake of the head. But even the ones who might have wanted to help could give him no information. After trying the town's livery stables, Griff felt fairly certain that Ed Luft must still be in town.

It was just at dusk, while men carried ladders up and down the length of Harrison Avenue to light the gas street lamps, that he ran into Mike Malloy and Frank Gower in a bar that was frequented by striking miners. They were eager to find out what progress he had made in finding Ed Luft, but he gave a negative response to every one of their questions. Malloy swore under his breath. "We been trying to find out something about your man, Luft, on our own. Seems we owe you that much after what you've done for us. But we only draw a blank."

Gower suggested, "You suppose you put such a scare in him—almost running him down that way—that he's still running?"

Griff shook his head. "I've had another look at that

place on State Street where you sent me last night—Drago's. There seems to be a room or two at the back, for private games maybe. I was just wondering . . ."

Malloy took that up. "You think Luft may be hiding out there? By God, there's one way to find out!"

"By rounding up your men and hitting Drago's? You'd end up battling that whole crowd of toughs." Griff shook his head. "I wouldn't want to get you in trouble on my account. You've got enough trouble of your own. But I thank you all the same."

He also appreciated the fact that they had never once asked him his reasons for wanting to find Ed Luft. He hated keeping friends in the dark, but he couldn't do any different without admitting his true identity.

It was nearly midnight when Griff returned to his hotel, his mood heavy. Leadville was noisy even at this chill hour, but the hotel lobby was empty. He took his key from its hook on the board behind the desk and climbed to his room. He turned the key in the lock and entered, leaving the door open for light to help him find the lamp on the table. When he dug up a match and got the wick going, the flame wavered briefly under the draft from an open window.

Even as the glass chimney clinked into place, he remembered that he had left that window shut.

The warning thought came too late. The sound of a gun going to full cock brought his head around quickly; the glow of the lamp showed him the man who sat comfortably on the bed, his back propped against the headboard, the gun in his fist pointed squarely at Griff.

"I'd begun to wonder if you was gonna show," Ed Luft told him.

Jaw muscles tightening, Griff looked into the black gun muzzle.

Not waiting for an answer, Luft went on, gesturing with his gun barrel, "First thing I want is the gun I know you got under that coat. Lift it out real careful, and let's have it here on the bed."

There was no point in resisting, though it infuriated Griff to have to obey. He tossed the weapon onto the bed, and Luft stretched out a hand and snaked it closer to him. Now that Luft's prisoner was disarmed, his next thought was for the hall door, which was still standing open. "Back up," he ordered. "Slow! Shut the door without turning around—and don't even think about trying to duck out on me. And then pull that chair over here, where I can see you good, and have a seat. We got some talking to do."

The menacing eye of the revolver followed Griff's every move. When he had taken his place, seated stiffly on the straight-backed chair, the two men looked at each other for a silent moment. It was Griff who finally said, "You led me on quite a chase."

"How the hell did you find me?"

"Your trail was easy enough to follow. You scattered your share of the loot across Montana and Wyoming like you couldn't wait to get it spent. People remembered that, and remembered *you*. I guess you didn't realize I could give a good description of that red beard of yours, which the mask didn't more than halfway cover."

Luft's eyes narrowed, and his face hardened under its patch of wiry whiskers; but he said nothing. Griff went on, "Finally I met a woman in a saloon at Laramie. You told her your name, and also that you knew a place to get more money when that ran out—by helping busting up a miners' strike in Leadville. That was all I needed to know."

"That little bitch!" Luft grunted. "I might have known she couldn't keep her mouth shut."

"That was you who followed me up here to my room from Drago's last night, wasn't it?" Griff asked.

"Yep. You thought I wouldn't recognize you during the row on Fryer Hill without that mustache, didn't you?"

Griff touched a finger to the unfamiliar, smooth skin of his upper lip. "I had another reason for doing that," he said grimly. "Thanks to you and your friends, I've got the express company after me!"

"Oh?" If anything, Luft seemed amused to hear it. "Now is that a fact?"

"It damn well is! After that stage job in Montana, they had a man on the case in no time at all—a man named Showalt, a tough one to deal with. He figured it had to have been an inside job, and since Burke, the shotgunner, was dead, that left me. I couldn't make Showalt believe I'd heard Burke yell out the name of one of the holdup men, just before he was shot—a name that sounded to me like 'Milo.' It turned out none of the stage passengers had been close enough to hear, or to back up my story. Showalt was sure I'd made it all up, to try and save my own skin by switching the blame onto a dead man."

Luft's mouth quirked. "Burke was nothing but a fool! He tried to hold out for a bigger cut than we offered him. He ended up getting nothing at all."

"In other words," Griff said coldly, "you didn't need him for anything more, so Milo shot him down while you held a gun on me—and the three of you split Burke's share between you. Is that about the shape of it?"

The bearded man returned his look without expression. The gun remained unwavering as he snapped, "Get on with your story. What about the detective?"

Griff Cameron shrugged. "He made a mistake, probably the one and only time he ever did. I guess he was too sure of me; he turned careless for a minute and I got away. But I haven't the slightest doubt that he's somewhere on my track right now—his kind would never give up on a man who pulled a thing like that on him! I figured my only chance was to find the ones who did that job, try to bring them in, and clear myself. It was hard work, but I managed to hit on *your* trail. What happened to the others?"

"You mean Milo and Steeger? As if I'd tell you—even if I knew!" But then Luft carelessly went on, "When we divided the take and split up, they mentioned heading for Oregon. Or was it California? Hell, I don't remember. Either way, they're long gone by this time."

It was no more than he had expected to hear, but it hit Griff hard. He had been lucky to have picked up on even one of the outlaws, he supposed. The man before him now had been his single hope.

Ed Luft seemed to read his thought. He said heavily, "So I guess this makes you *my* problem, don't it, Cameron?"

Meeting his stare, looking into the unwavering muzzle of the gun, Griff felt the full weight of heavy irony: He had picked up the trail and followed it so many miles, clear to Leadville, only to have Ed Luft turn the tables and take him completely by surprise. He drew a breath and said harshly, "Then what's holding you back? All you have to do is pull the trigger."

Luft gave a scornful snort. "Here? In a hotel room? That's likely, ain't it? There's better places." He swung his legs over the bed and came around the foot of it, the gun trained steadily on his prisoner. "Get on your feet," he ordered, "and get away from that chair!"

Griff slowly obeyed, his hands in the clear. He watched the bearded man boot the chair out of his path, and then they stood confronted, their stares locked.

"We're going to leave," Luft announced, "and you'll be ahead of me. Do anything to force my hand, and we'll finish our business right quick." Having issued that warning, he jerked his head toward the door.

Aware of the man behind him and of the revolver aimed at his back, Griff crossed to the door and opened it on the lighted, empty hallway. He could hear the sound of muffled snores behind the panels that lined the corridor.

In his mind Griff Cameron pictured the steps leading down to the empty lobby, the street entrance, and the veranda that lay beyond. Suddenly a thought struck him. He was remembering this morning . . . the tough who had been trailing Mike Malloy . . . the gun he had taken off the man and tossed under the porch steps. His mind worked furiously, wondering if the gun was still there and if he could possibly get his hands on it; any chance was better than letting himself be marched away to his own murder. His breathing was shallow as he started for the stairwell.

At once the hard muzzle of the gun dug into the meat of his back. "Not that way!" Luft said softly. "Hell, d'you think I'd take you right out through the lobby? Just keep walking!"

Griff saw the chance he had hoped for, poor as it was, fade away. They continued on silently between the rows of closed doors. At the corridor's end, they turned into a shorter hallway and came to a door that Luft ordered Griff to open. They stepped through onto the head of a flight of wooden steps that angled away down the dark, outside wall of the building.

A night wind breathed against them, plucking at the hem of Griff's coat. Beyond the lower buildings adjoining the two-storied hotel, the glow of gas street lamps lit up the night sky; by contrast, the stairs below them dropped past darkened windows, toward almost total blackness.

Griff heard the door click into place behind them, shutting away the faint glimmer of light from the hall they had just left. Luft spoke gruffly in his ear: "All right. Down you go . . ." His hand on the railing, Griff felt for the dropoff of the first step.

His captor was close behind him as he descended a half dozen steps. Then a sudden curse and scrape of boots told him Luft had missed his footing briefly in the dark. Griff didn't hesitate. Back muscles braced and half expecting the blast of the revolver to blow a hole through him, he doubled over and swung aside, still grasping the handrail.

The weight of the other man slammed full against him, and Luft gave a startled yell. For some reason the gun failed to go off, but Griff felt it strike a glancing blow against his arm. He released his hold on the railing and made a wild grab for the weapon. His fingers closed on it and on Luft's fist, which held the gun, but then he lost his grip and closed down on the wrist instead. Next moment, struggling, they both fell.

Their combined weight struck the flimsy railing, but somehow it held and they bounced off it, against the rough clapboards of the wall. After that, in a wild tangle, they were plummeting and rolling down the steps. Griff took a hard knock on the back of his skull, sending skyrockets bursting through his head; somehow he managed to grapple with his enemy and keep his hold on the wrist that held the gun. Then the weapon went off, and he felt the man's arm shake from the explosion, but he wasn't aware of the bullet striking him anywhere.

Griff hardly knew when the confused and bruising tumble abruptly came to a stop. Dazed, his skull throbbing, he seemed to be lying on his back with his legs higher than his head and a heavy weight across him. The darkness had ceased its spinning, and everything was still. After a moment of this, a sense of urgency broke through the numbness and forced him to gather his wits and his strength. He wasn't sure how he managed to drag himself free of the burden that lay across him, but he at last kicked free. Breathing heavily, he rolled himself to hands and knees and after another moment pushed to his feet. He put out a hand, felt the roughness of clapboards, and leaned his weight against them as he waited for his head to clear.

He became aware of doors slamming, of shouting voices and nearing footsteps. Drawn by the disturbance, men in varying stages of undress were cautiously approaching this slot between adjoining buildings. One or two carried oil lamps they had snatched up. By this wavering light he looked at the upturned, bearded face and the staring eyes of Ed Luft—and the darkly spreading stain of blood across the man's chest.

Someone yelled hoarsely, "Hell! We got another killing!"

Turning, Griff looked at the forms and faces crowding

about him. He was still too dazed to do much more than stare, and too dazed to resist when hands fell upon him and held him fast. Lamplight gleamed on the twin barrels of a shotgun, and he heard the man who held it issuing orders: "Leave things just the way they are. Somebody go get the marshal. The rest of us will hold him until the law gets here. . . ."

Chapter Nine

The hands on the wall clock in the marshal's office showed one when the lawman entered, bringing the chill of the mountain air with him. He nodded to his deputy, who was dozing over a copy of the *Police Gazette*. He took off his hat, depositing it on a nail beside the door, and then ran his bony fingers through his tight, grizzled hair. He asked his man, "Is the prisoner awake?"

The deputy put down his paper. "So far as I know."

"Even if he isn't, wake him up and bring him in here."

Griff Cameron was not asleep; in spite of the hour, he'd felt little inclination for sleep. When he came out of his cell, it was to find Jud Osland seated at the flattopped desk, sunk deep into his chair with shoulders hunched and fingers laced across his gaunt middle. The lawman scowled at Griff from under bushy brows and nodded toward the chair opposite. As the prisoner took a seat, Osland told his deputy, "You can take a hike, Wilbur. I want to talk to him."

The night deputy hesitated, reluctant to obey. "You best be careful. He's already killed one man tonight." But the marshal flapped a bony hand at him, and with a shrug Wilbur took his hat and jacket and went out into the night, closing the door softly behind him. There was almost no sound then, except for the slow beat of the pendulum moving the works inside the clock on the office wall.

The jail was in the oldest section of town, on Front Street, at the very edge of the flat overlooking California Gulch, where Leadville had begun. Here, the town's raucous nighttime voice seemed far away and muted. The two men regarded each other wordlessly for long minutes, Griff Cameron waiting for the marshal to come out with whatever he had to say. Finally, the marshal shifted his position with a sigh.

"All right," he said heavily after learning his prisoner's name. "We'll begin at the top. Is this your gun?"

He took the weapon from the drawer and laid it on the desk, between them. It was an ancient Colt revolver with a scarred wooden handle. Griff recognized it as the one he had stared into during his talk with Ed Luft, the one that had taken its owner's life during their confused tumble down the steps. He shook his head no. "Mine's a forty-five Smith and Wesson. Last time I saw it, it was lying on the bed in my hotel room."

"This one, maybe?" Osland produced another gun from the drawer and laid it beside Luft's. He looked at Griff, who nodded. The marshal closed the drawer, leaving the guns on the desk. From the casual way he did it, Griff knew that both weapons were unloaded. He waited.

The marshal put the tips of bony fingers together and looked over them at his prisoner. "Let's back up a few hours," he said crisply, "to this afternoon, when I seen you chasing a man away from that affair on Harrison. You lost him that time. But it would look like you finally caught up with him—and got what you wanted."

"That was far from what I wanted," Griff corrected him. "I was after information, but he decided I needed killing. I tried to wrestle the gun out of his hand. You see how it ended."

"I see." Osland looked skeptical. "Are you ready to tell me what this information is about?"

Griff shook his head. "No."

The marshal scratched at beard stubble, fingers digging into his lean cheeks. "You know you ain't doing yourself any favors, trying to play closemouthed with the law!"

"I suppose not. But this was a personal matter. Nothing I can discuss."

There was a long pause. The clock ticked away, and a pine stick snapped and settled in the potbellied stove, which was burning to take off some of the late-night chill. "So your mind's made up, is it?" the lawman said heavily. When Griff merely returned his look, Osland went on, "Well, now, it happens I've been doing some checking on my own, and I've managed to find out a few things that you could have told me and saved me the trouble. I've learned the man's name was Ed Luft, and that he was here on account of this damn strike. Is that also what brought you?"

Again Griff shook his head. "It was something entirely different. Something that happened a long way from here."

"Meaning, it's none of my business?"

"Not as marshal of Leadville."

That careful statement got him a cold stare as the lawman tried to interpret its meaning. Osland swore suddenly and slapped one bony palm against the desktop. "You ain't helping me at all, Cameron. Looks like I'll have to piece this thing together for myself." He raised a lean finger, to tick off each point. "First, a man was killed tonight. Second, there were no witnesses. Third . . ." He pointed at the wooden-handled Colt lying between them. "Did you happen to notice this?"

Puzzled, Griff picked up the gun and turned it to the light for a better look. Among the scratches on the wooden handle, he found he could make out letters, scored there by a knife blade—the initials "EL".

"Luft was apparently killed by his own gun," the marshal continued, "tussling with an unarmed man who'd left his own pistol in his room. And for reasons," Osland added dryly, "that ain't supposed to be none of my business!" He swore again and swung his lanky shape out of the chair. He paced a couple of strides, returned, and scowled at the other man.

"Maybe you'll tell me this much," he said suddenly. "If I turn you loose, who else in my town do you suppose you'll be killing? Intentional or otherwise?"

Griff was caught off guard, but he quickly recovered. "Nobody else," he said flatly. "Ed Luft was the only one I was interested in here—and I never meant to kill *him*. He was my last chance." He was unable to keep an edge of bitterness from his voice. "I wanted him *alive*. . . ."

The marshal seemed to reach a decision. "All right. Take your gun and get out of my office. I'm letting you go," he said gruffly, "for lack of evidence. Besides, I never did care a hell of a lot for strikebreakers! But let me give you some advice. Maybe you better not waste too much more time here in Leadville. I'm likely to catch hell for what I'm doing—the men who hire the likes of Ed Luft carry the weight in this town. If you ain't around, I won't have to defy a direct order to go out and arrest you again. You understand me?"

Griff was on his feet, still not quite believing that he was a free man. "I understand," he said. "I more than appreciate this. Hope you don't have cause to regret it."

"You don't hope it any worse than I do," Osland told him gruffly. He pointed at the door. "That's the way out." He was scowling heavily, as though still debating the wisdom of what he had done, when Griff stepped into the night and pulled the door shut behind him.

Griff's hotel room was just as he had left it, except that in his absence someone had closed the window, blown out the lamp, and shut the door. He half expected to find his belongings rifled or missing, but everything seemed intact. He locked the door with the key, which he still had in his pocket. Next, seated on the edge of the bed, he plugged fresh loads from his pack into the Smith and Wesson. He felt a shade easier when the gun was no longer empty.

But only for an instant. The aftermath of all that had recently happened suddenly washed over him. Without undressing or taking off his boots, he stretched out on the bed with his gun beside him and stared at the ceiling, thoughts and emotions numbed except for an awareness of failure, like a knot at the core of him.

With that killing tonight, the last door had slammed in his face. No longer could he hope that Ed Luft would confess and clear him of a part in that robbery; and Luft hadn't been able even to suggest where to hunt for his vanished partners, Milo and Steeger. By now they had disappeared into the vastness of the West—and Griff was left with a charge of robbery and of complicity in the killing of the stage guard hanging over him.

At any moment he expected to hear the tramp of boots in the corridor and a knock at his door, announcing the marshal, ready to haul him back to jail for the murder of Ed Luft. If it came to that, he knew Jud Osland—coerced by the powers in the town into arresting him—would be performing an onerous duty and that it would be unfair to resist. Just now he didn't much care what happened.

His eyes closed, and when he opened them again it was to find the streaky light of morning filling the room.

The lamp on the table had burned itself almost empty. When with a groan he dropped his feet off the bed and pushed himself up, he was sharply aware of every blow and knock he had taken in that tumble down the steps with Ed Luft. Flexing his muscles, he thought with a grimace, *Maybe this is what it feels like to get old!* After putting out the lamp, he stripped off his soiled shirt and washed up; the touch of cold water seemed to clear his head. As he laid out his shaving materials, his thoughts were already busy with what lay ahead.

Had anyone wanted his hide for killing Ed Luft, he would have heard about it by now, he figured. Perhaps Luft had been too minor a figure to matter to those who had hired him for use against the strikers. Still, there was no sense pressing his luck by staying in town another day; but he would not go sneaking out of the place, whatever Morgan Slaughter and his bullyboy, Tom Riordan, might have to say. He intended to leave with dignity.

So it was that later, after a leisurely breakfast, Griff walked unhurriedly through Leadville's streets, openly carrying his bag. There was one call he felt a need to make before going to the stage station. When he arrived at Mike Malloy's shack, the place showed all its poverty, standing in weeds in a row of other, similar shanties. A thread of smoke rising from the chimney indicated that someone was at home, but when he knocked, he got no immediate answer. He waited and then knocked again.

The door opened—narrowly, at first, until Mike Malloy recognized his visitor. Then he threw it wide, his face blank with astonishment. "You!" he stammered. "We heard you was in jail!"

"News travels in this town, doesn't it?"

Malloy moved aside, making room for his visitor, and saying, "Come in! Come in!"

But Griff shook his head. "I can't," he said. "I only stopped by." So the Irishman stepped out instead, drawing the door closed behind him, but not before Griff saw half a dozen other men, crowded around the table in the shack's main room. They bore the appearance of miners, and he said, "Looks almost like a council of war in there."

Malloy's face was bleak. "You talk about news traveling? The rumors are really flying this morning! They say Tabor's sent a wire to the governor. We don't know what for. There's some who say he's asked for martial law . . . or maybe guns, enough to outfit a private army to use against us. Anyway, we're trying to decide what we can do about it."

"Maybe it is just a rumor," Griff suggested. "Has there been any further trouble because of you defying that letter?"

Malloy shook his head. "I think it's like you said. Morgan Slaughter made a public show of calling the dogs off me, and for the time being I guess he has to live with it, to keep up appearances. But no way of knowing how long that will last."

"I don't have to tell you to be careful."

"Hardly! But what about you? The word is that you killed somebody last night. Was it Ed Luft?"

"Yes," Griff confirmed. "It was an unlucky accident. Your marshal arrested me but then turned me loose again. It's my impression he doesn't care a lot for the way the owners are treating this strike, but he's not in a place where he can do much about it. He did say it might be a good idea for me not to stay around long—for my own good."

Malloy eyed the bag in Griff's hand. "Looks like you're taking his advice. Well, probably all for the best, seeing some of the enemies you've made for yourself."

"I'm taking the morning stage. I didn't feel like going without saying good-bye—and wishing you luck."

"Sure, an' I'm wishing you the same," the Irishman agreed wholeheartedly. He thrust out a work-hardened hand. "I'll never be forgettin' you stepped in to help me, when there was no call that you should. I only wish I'd been able to make it up to you."

"Don't worry about it," Griff said as their hands met.

It was apparent to Nan Harper that once again the stage line was going to lose money on the morning run to Georgetown. Only one fare had been sold, to a drummer who now sat impatiently on a bench in the station waiting for the coach to be under way, his samples case beside him. Of course, the driver would make his customary swing by the Clarendon Hotel on the way out of town—Jerry Dobbins occasionally was able to pick up a passenger there. But that seemed to happen less often as word got around that the Harper line was a hard-luck outfit whose livestock sometimes went lame and whose ancient stagecoach was known, on occasion, to break down.

The drummer, a fussy little man with long, flowing sideburns, pulled out a pocket watch and checked it with the office clock. "Miss," he said anxiously, "I thought we'd be leaving by now. You see the time?"

"Yes, I know," she told him. "The boys should be just about ready to hitch up. If you'll excuse me, I'll step outside and see how they're doing."

She put aside her pen, closed the ledger she was working on, and gave the man a reassuring smile; then she hurried out, praying that Jerry and Dick hadn't run into problems.

The old coach stood forlornly in the yard, battle scarred from its many miles on hard trails. Jerry, prepared and ready to climb to his seat and take the reins, had made a last-minute inspection and found an axle box that needed attention. Now he was on his knees beside the wheel, grease bucket handy, working at the messy job, which should have been tended to earlier. Yonder, Dick Walsh was bringing up the harnessed team, with leather straps dragging and ready to snap into place.

One of the horses was giving him trouble. It was a roan, a veteran like the old stagecoach—a tough animal with a jaw of iron and a mean disposition, who seldom willingly surrendered to the cruel necessity of going to work but fought it as a matter of principle.

Unfortunately, the big roan knew it had Dick Walsh buffaloed. Dick, a slight and gangly fellow, was frightened of the animal—something a horse can always sense in a person who tries to handle it. Coming up from the corral, the roan was setting its heels in the dirt and tossing its head, trying to jerk the bridle out of the young fellow's hand—and perhaps pull his arm from the socket. Dick yelled at the roan in an angry voice shaking with barely disguised terror; the horse circled and trumpeted as the dust rose under its hooves. Jerry, familiar with this occurrence, swore and threw down the rag he was using to go lend a hand.

At that moment Nan saw a man walk into the yard in the bright sunlight.

Turning, she threw up a hand to shade her eyes, enabling her to get a better look at him. When she noticed the bag he carried, she was sure she was looking at another fare and gave a sigh of satisfaction. But when he drew nearer and lifted his head, she made out the face that had been shaded by his hat brim; it was Griff Cameron—and much to her surprise she experienced a quick stab of disappointment with the realization that he was leaving.

She was keenly aware of everything about him in that moment, the way he walked, the competent set of his shoulders, the balance of his head, and his definite masculinity. But there was something else about him, just now—a troubled air that made her frown in sudden sympathy, wondering what it could be that bothered him.

He returned her greeting, set down his bag, and straightened, saying, "I was afraid I might have missed the morning stage."

Nan indicated the coach. "Not yet. But you didn't need to worry, in any case. We're not the only line in operation."

"I know," he said, and smiled briefly. "But if you did have a coach going out, that was the one I wanted to take."

"Thank you." She hesitated. "Are you leaving Leadville, then?"

"It appears that way. I've got no reason to stay here now."

Nan's dark eyes turned toward her feet. Then she looked up at him and said, "Frankly, I've been a little concerned about you, since yesterday. I hope that man Riordan hasn't made any more trouble."

Griff shook his head. "Not after your friend Slaughter told him where to head in. It seemed to do the trick."

"That's good. Except—" She felt her cheeks grow warm with faint embarrassment, because she felt compelled to set the record straight. "Except that Morgan Slaughter isn't exactly my friend. In fact, I don't like him at all. But I feel I should at least try to be polite on Grandpa's account. . . ."

A squeal from an angry horse interrupted her. Jerry and the other boy, between them, had the team settled; but now, as they started leading the animals on toward the coach, the roan started acting up again worse than ever. In a confusion of rearing and yelling and slamming of hooves, dust rose to envelop humans and animals alike. Suddenly, out of that cloud, the form of Jerry Dobbins was propelled with arms flailing, and he hit the ground in a limp heap. Nan gave a choked scream, her hands flying to her face. But by then Griff had left her and was running toward the disaster.

Just as quickly as it had begun acting up, the roan appeared to have settled. By the time Nan reached Jerry, Griff was already there, kneeling in the dust beside the young driver, who lay sprawled on his back, eyes closed and cheeks colorless, his breathing quick and shallow. Griff was working at the buttons of Jerry's shirt and laying it open, baring his chest. Lying there, the driver looked very young and vulnerable; already the beginnings of an angry bruise were beginning to form on his chest. Griff felt the injured area with careful fingers, and when he lifted his eyes to Nan's, his expression was sober.

"The boy is hurt pretty bad. It will take a doctor to say just how bad. The blow caught him dead center. It may have got a couple of ribs."

Nan bit her lip, unable to speak. Now her grandfather came limping hurriedly from the direction of the barn. His thinning hair stood out from his head, and his eyes were wild with shock. Bill Harper looked in bewilderment at the figure on the ground and the others gathered about it. "What in the world's happened?" he demanded.

Nan found her voice. "It's the roan! The boys were having trouble with him, and he—" She indicated the hurt boy with a helpless gesture.

The old man's chest swelled. He cried, "I'm gonna get my rifle! We've put up with that brute when he should of been destroyed a long time ago—before he had a chance to do something like *this*!"

"Mr. Harper! No!" Dick Walsh cried in a tone of anguish. "Don't blame the roan—it's *my* fault. I just don't rightly know how to handle him. But he's a damn good team horse. Honest! You mustn't shoot him!"

They all looked at the boy. His face had gone colorless, and there was a shine of tears in his eyes. Oddly enough, as though the roan had got all the orneriness out of its system, it stood docilely now beside its teammate, giving no trouble at all. Seeing this, Harper turned away with a shake of the head and helplessly flung out his hands.

Nan looked again at Jerry, lying hurt and unconscious. "We can't leave him here like this, in the dirt!"

"That's a fact," Griff said, and got to his feet. "Where do you want him put?"

Nan's grandfather scratched at his gray-stubbled jaw; he seemed bewildered and unable to cope with what was happening around him. It was Nan who suggested, "We've got an army cot set up in the office."

"Fine!" Griff nodded. "Show me where it is. We can use the cot for a stretcher—we have to be very careful about moving him."

They hurried to get it. Nan realized she had forgotten all about the drummer, who now stood in the doorway staring at the scene in the yard and holding his samples case. He started to stammer a question, but she rushed by him with an apologetic shake of the head. Standing near the wood stove beyond the railing, the cot was made up with a pillow and blankets; it was used whenever someone had to stay in the office overnight. Griff picked it up easily enough, and Nan held the partition gate open while he carried the cot outside, where Dick now had the horses in place at the stagecoach and hurried to lend a hand.

He and Griff gently lifted the hurt man onto the cot, then picked it up and carried it and its limp burden into the building. Nan and her grandfather followed them in. As soon as the cot had been set down, Griff told Dick, "Next thing we need is for you to fetch a doctor—just as fast as you can find one."

The young man hesitated, protesting, "I got to finish hitching up. . . ."

"What for?" Bill Harper retorted heavily. "We ain't making any run today."

The drummer, who had kept back out of the way during all this activity, let out a bleat of protest. "What are you saying? How about *me*? I got my ticket. I been waiting all this time."

Nan's heart ached as she saw the defeat in her grandfather's face. Bill said, "I'm sorry, mister. Your money will be refunded. With my driver laid up, that's the best I can do."

"Maybe it ain't!" Dick spoke up, almost stammering in his eagerness. "Let *me* take this run!"

Bill looked at him. "You? Don't be silly."

"I mean it! So maybe I ain't never driven one of these, but I'm game to try! Anything's better than canceling," he insisted. "Look—none of the outfits could roll yesterday, while that slide was being cleared. That means business will be backed up and waiting at Georgetown. We can't afford not to get our share." But he stopped his speech at the adamant shake of the old man's head; he should have known he would be refused. He'd been told before by Bill Harper that he lacked the size and the wrists and—most importantly—the training to take on driving a coach across the Mosquitos.

Nan understood then what she had to do. She took the old man's arm to draw his attention. "Grandpa," she said, "*I* can do it. I know I can!" She went on quickly, not giving him time to refuse. "I've ridden the box, lots of times—and years back I used to tease the drivers until they'd let me take over the ribbons and give me lessons. Look!" She spread her hands; they had always seemed unfeminine and huge to her. "Lord knows I'm strong enough, and big enough! You can't deny it."

He gave her a hurt look, and she knew what he was thinking. All her life, Nan's grandfather had insisted on seeing in her an image of her tiny and graceful mother and, despite the evidence, had refused to listen to her protests that she was nothing like that at all—that she was awkward and outsized and plain. Now his voice fairly rang with indignation as he stiffened and told her firmly, "You are my granddaughter! I never raised you to be like Calamity Jane or any of them unwomanly females. *You*— drive a stage? No, sir. You're a lady. I won't have you doing a man's job, and that's final!"

"But Grandpa!" she cried. "How can we run a stage line without a driver?"

His face was like iron; he had closed his mind and would not hear. She gave up then, defeated . . . only to hear Griff Cameron say, in quiet tones, "It's all right, Nan. You got a driver." And as she turned slowly to stare at him, he added, "Mr. Harper, the other day you offered me a job. If the offer's still open, I'd like to take it."

Old Bill Harper looked thunderstruck, new hope struggling against his despair. Mouth suddenly trembling, he pointed out, "You understand that I can't pay top wages. . . ."

"Let's not worry about that now. Here's a coach that has to get on the road. And a man who needs a doctor."

A practical person, Nan quickly accepted the change of affairs. To young Dick Walsh, she exclaimed, "Grandpa already told you to go find one. Don't worry about the horses—I can finish hitching up." She almost had to give the youngster a shove before he came to life and with a

nod went rushing off. Nan turned then to the drummer.
"Sir, you should be on your way in just a few minutes.
And I do want to thank you. You've been very patient."

The man appeared mollified. He made a gesture and
mumbled something about emergencies happening. As for
Griff, he seemed impatient now to get on with the job for
which he'd volunteered, but Bill Harper held him a moment longer. It touched Nan to see the tears of gratitude
in her grandfather's eyes, and to hear the humility and
gratitude with which he insisted, "Mr. Cameron, you can't
know how much it means to me for you to do this."

Griff told him briefly, "As this gent says, emergencies
sometimes change a lot of things. . . ."

But Nan could not let the matter rest with that. As
she and Griff left the office together to finish readying the
coach, she said, "I'm afraid I don't understand. You have
your own problems. Why should you drop everything else
on our account?"

Griff stopped and turned to face her. "I meant what I
told your grandfather. When someone you like needs help—
help that you're able to give—it seems the only thing to
do."

"Have you any idea how long you can stay?"

"Long enough, I hope, to have Jerry on his feet and
able to do his job again." He hesitated, and she sensed
there was more, something that he found difficult to tell
her. Then it came: "Nan, I didn't tell your grandfather
. . . but it's only fair that you should know. There are
reasons why I might have to pick up and leave, almost at a
moment's notice. Much as I'd hate to leave you short-
handed, I want you to be prepared."

She frowned, studying his expression; tall for a woman,
she still had to tilt her head a trifle to meet his serious
glance. Anxious questions were poised on her tongue; she
wanted to blurt out, "Then you *are* in trouble!" But she
swallowed the words—there was something in the attractive but secretive man that forbade too easy an intimacy.
She could only nod and say earnestly, "I thank you for

telling me this. If that's how it works out, we'll deal with
it."

His face softened in a smile. "It's important to me
that we understand each other. Now what do you say we
get on with the job?"

Chapter Ten

Driving for the Harper Stage Line was almost the last job Griff Cameron would have wanted, or expected to see himself take on. Certain that Showalt, the detective from the express company, could not be far behind, Griff knew he should have been putting distance between them—not sitting on the box of a rattletrap stagecoach and tooling it over treacherous mountain roads, waiting for the regular driver to recover. But even though the promise he had made was a rash one, walking away and leaving Nan and her grandfather in their predicament was somehow impossible for him to do.

Now, after four days on the job, he understood the problems facing the Harper Stage Line. In better times, Bill Harper would have been sending out a coach to Georgetown every morning, the year round. Today, three round trips per week were enough to set a grueling pace for the company's sole driver and his teams, and for the old stagecoach, the only vehicle still in running order. Such was the condition to which a once-prosperous stage and freight company had been reduced by changing times, by Bill Harper's medical expenses, and by pressure from competitors.

Having long since lost their mail franchise, the best

115

the Harpers could do now was try to catch the overflow of passengers the other companies couldn't handle; all too often the old stage rolled near to empty. And to compound the problem, Bill was no longer able to maintain stations for changing teams along the sixty-mile route, and he had to pay exorbitant fees to rival companies to stable his animals. The ten dollars per passenger the stage line took in was barely enough to keep wages and feed bills paid and equipment in repair.

When he started the return journey to Leadville that morning, Griff Cameron had a couple of fares he had managed to pick up when the train from Denver pulled into the Georgetown depot. It was an uneasy moment for him, waiting beside his coach while he scanned the faces of those getting off the train—looking, always, for one face he didn't want to see.

He had a fatalistic certainty that sooner or later one of those travelers would bear the familiar, hawkish features of Vern Showalt. The express company detective had a reputation of never giving up once he settled on something he wanted; he would never let up on a man who had given him the slip and escaped. One of these days he would be stepping off that train from Denver. And when he did—when the two of them met face to face—the inevitable confrontation would occur.

But this was not the day, and once he was on the road again, Griff let himself relax. Since the holdup that had turned his life upside down and made him a fugitive, he had known few restful hours. But on the seat of a stagecoach, away from staring eyes, he could enjoy for a time the familiar routine of turning wheels and plodding hooves, the feel of the leathers in his hands—and in his lungs, the thin, chill air here at the roof of the world.

There could be peace in this empty loneliness. Unfortunately there was also time to work at the useless treadmill of his thoughts.

It began to look as though fate had dealt him a rotten hand. During his search for Ed Luft there had always been at least a kind of hope. That hope had ended with the unlucky bullet that killed the red-bearded outlaw; now Griff was left with nothing more than two names, Milo and Steeger—names of men who had long since vanished into regions of which even their partner, Luft, had had no clue. Washington, Oregon—it hardly mattered. That was a trail gone completely cold by now. A man could spend the rest of a lifetime roaming the West and not expect to pick it up again.

Well, in life a man had to play the cards he held; he wasn't able to toss them in the discard and ask for a second deal. Such was the conclusion Griff always came back to during these sessions on the seat of a swaying stagecoach, alone with his thoughts.

And in spite of everything, when he drove the coach down out of the higher reaches of the hills and saw Leadville lying spread out on the flat below him, he felt a lift of spirits . . . and he had an idea it was because he would soon be seeing Nan Harper.

Today, having dropped his fares at the Clarendon, he rolled on to the stage-line yard and halted before the office. Dick Walsh came hurrying from the barn, and Griff returned his greeting and tiredly swung down from the box, turning the outfit over to the yardman.

Old Bill Harper had come out of the office and was waiting for him on the porch. Griff climbed the steps, whipping trail dust from his clothing with the brim of his hat. His first question was, "How's Jerry?"

"Doing all right, it looks like. Doctor hasn't got him doped up anymore against the pain. We still have him at our house, of course, where Nan can look after him."

"What's the doctor say?"

"That we're giving him the right treatment. Of course, it takes time to mend after punishment like that."

"Yeah."

Griff hadn't expected to hear anything different. It was obvious he couldn't look for any sudden release from the promise that held him here. He nodded when Harper suggested, "Come inside and tell me about the run."

He dropped his bag beside the cot, this being his sleeping quarters now. Afterward, seated beside Bill's ancient desk, Griff made his brief report on the condition of the road and the uneventful trip, and handed over the twenty dollars he had collected from his two passengers. Bill gave the money a long and sober look and then shrugged as he said heavily, "Not much, but better than nothing."

He took a tin cash box from the desk drawer where he kept it, added the silver and greenbacks to its meager contents, scribbled a note of deposit, and replaced the box in its drawer. "And it looks like it'll *be* nothing, pretty soon." He wagged his head at Griff's questioning look. "The railroad's coming! Word has it the rails will be laid and the first train will be here in Leadville before July is out."

"That early?" Griff exclaimed. And he thought, *So even you have to admit—finally—that it's really going to happen!*

Harper nodded. Rubbing a palm over his gray-stubbled cheeks, he went on in the same lifeless voice, "Nobody will ride a stage when they can take the train all the way from Denver!" All at once he was blinking hard against tears, and the blue-veined hand at his cheek began to tremble.

Griff touched the old man's shoulder. "Bill, it's not the end of the world," he insisted. "Leadville isn't the only place to do business. After all, trains can't go everywhere, not yet at any rate, not for a long time to come. There'll still be room for stagecoach lines to run from end-of-track, not only in Colorado but in other places, too. Arizona, for one—where you wouldn't have to buck the kind of winters you've been putting up with all these years."

Harper raised an anguished face. "You're saying all I got to do is tear myself loose from all I've ever known.

Pick up everything and move to a new place and start from scratch. Is that what you mean?" His features twisted. "Griff, I'm too *old*! I wouldn't know how to start over. Anyway, it don't matter about me," he went on when the other man tried to interrupt. "It's Nan! I've hoped all along I was going to be able to leave her something. But now . . . what's gonna become of her, Griff?"

His distress was so apparent that Griff hastened to reassure him. "I wouldn't worry too much about Nan. She'll get along. She's a resourceful lady, with a good head on her shoulders."

"I know that. But to try to rebuild a stage line, from nothing—that's too big a job!" Suddenly Harper raised his head, and a thoughtful look appeared in his faded eyes, as though something had just struck him. He said, "You know we'll always be grateful, the way you've stepped in to help us with Jerry laid up. I know it wasn't nothing you had a mind to do, and I'll never be able to repay you. But . . . could I interest you in a partnership?"

"*What?*"

In his earnestness, Bill Harper clutched the younger man's sleeve. "Look, I know what I'm offering ain't got a helluva lot of cash value right now. But if you really do believe this stage line would be worth reestablishing somewhere else—worth the trouble and work to make it pay— why I'd be more than willing to cut you in. Say for a third interest, depending on if Nan's agreeable, of course. And after I'm gone, it would be for you two to split between you."

For a moment Griff was speechless. One thing seemed clear: Nan hadn't told her grandfather about Griff's warning that they must be prepared to see him leave at almost any time. This made his refusal harder to put in words. All he could finally say was, "I wish I could at least consider taking you up on that. But I'm afraid it's out of the question."

"Oh." It hurt Griff to watch the brief flare of hope fade from the old man's eyes. Bill Harper, there in his

battered chair behind the desk, seemed to become a little
smaller, a little more defeated. "I guess the truth is, you
was only trying to make an old man feel better, with what
you said about there still being a chance to save something
of the stage line. Wasn't my aim to put you on the spot,
Griff, or rope you into something. Forget I mentioned it."

Griff groaned inwardly at his own clumsiness of speech.
"You misunderstand," he protested lamely. "I meant every word I said. Believe me. I really did."

But he knew his words now fell on deaf ears.

The Harpers lived in a modest frame house near the
stage-line office. Built tall and narrow, in the style of the
period, it boasted a bow window and some fretsaw work
under its eaves. The house showed the ravages of severe
Colorado winters, which had scored the paint from its
boards; even so, there was a neatness about it, and the
picket fence stood straight and true.

As Griff rode closer to the house, he saw that a
strange horse and buggy waited before the gate. Nan must
be entertaining. Griff hesitated briefly, but then he opened
the gate and went up the short walk to the door. When he
knocked, it was opened by Nan herself.

She seemed genuinely pleased to see him; as for
Griff, he thought she made a very pleasant sight in the
simple housedress and apron, her brown hair drawn back
and caught in a blue ribbon. He had heard her speak of
herself as plain and unattractive, but in his opinion she
had an honest kind of charm that, he admitted, he found
preferable to the aggressive femininity of her friend Baby
Doe.

"Oh, hello!" she exclaimed. "You must have got in
early. No problems for you this trip, I hope?"

"No problems," he assured her.

"Come in."

She made way for him, but as he stepped through the
door he hesitated, quickly drawing off his hat as he saw
the woman who was seated in a stiff chair by the living

room window, holding a cup and saucer. He said, "You've got company. I didn't mean to intrude."

"You're not." Nan quickly introduced him, adding, "This is Augusta Tabor. . . ."

As the name registered, Griff looked at the woman with new interest. He was curious to see the wife of the richest man in Leadville. She didn't look at all like someone who now lived in a Denver mansion on the wealth pouring out of Horace Tabor's silver mines. She appeared to be in her late forties, a hard-jawed woman and rather forbidding. Plainly dressed despite her husband's wealth, with austere features that didn't look much accustomed to smiling, she sat bolt upright on the edge of her chair, as though she might have a ramrod up her back, and regarded him coolly through blue-tinted spectacles.

Griff said to Nan, "Your grandfather tells me Jerry Dobbins is doing well. I thought I might look in on him."

"He's sleeping just now."

"Then I won't bother him. I'll try again later."

"Of course. Come back this evening, if you like."

"Thanks. Maybe I will." Hat in hand, he looked at Nan. His mind was full of the conversation he had just had with her grandfather. There were many things he wanted to discuss with her, but they would have to wait; this was obviously not the time. He made some final remark and nodded again to the older woman, and a moment later he was gone.

Nan stood in the door a moment, watching him close the gate after him and then pull on his hat as he regarded the livery-stable horse and rig that Augusta Tabor had left tied to an iron hitching post before the house. She saw how he gave the animal a pat on the neck before he turned downhill toward the center of town. She closed the door and turned back into the living room as her visitor commented, in dry Vermont tones, "He seems like a competent man. He works for you, does he?"

"Just the last few days," Nan answered. "He's filling in for Jerry Dobbins, our regular driver. I told you about

Jerry getting hurt." She resumed her place on the horse-hair sofa. "He's very capable."

"Jerry? He strikes me as little more than a boy."

"I meant Griff Cameron," Nan quickly corrected her. "Twice now, in the few days we've known him, he's stepped in during an emergency and helped us out. There really doesn't seem to be much he doesn't know about stage-coaching."

"Where did he work before?"

She found herself hesitating over the answer. "I'm not sure I know. He mentioned Arizona, though he didn't make it clear if that was the last place or not. In any event, it was a lucky day for us when he came to Leadville!"

That got her a look through the blue-tinted lenses. Augusta Tabor's mouth drew down slightly. "You sound very keen on the fellow, for someone you hardly even know. . . ."

Nan felt her cheeks grow warm. "Oh, I wouldn't say that!" she protested, too quickly.

Augusta's stern look was forbidding; she seemed to speak from some core of bitterness as she pointed out, "I can tell you that it's possible to be married to a man for over twenty years, and then wonder if you know him at all!" As soon as the words were spoken, she seemed to regret them. "I said more than I meant to, just then. You might find it hard to understand."

"It's none of my business," Nan said quickly. "You don't have to explain anything to me."

But Augusta said, "You're one of the very few whom I *could* explain it to. You're a sensible girl, one I've always felt comfortable with—one I was able to talk to."

Watching Augusta turn to set her coffee cup on the table by her chair, Nan found herself wondering, *Why? Because I'm someone who's as plain as you?* But she sensed that the older woman had something of which she wanted to unburden herself, and out of sympathy she waited.

"I hardly have any friends now," Augusta went on,

without prompting. "Certainly not among the people I've met since I've been in Denver! All they care about is their money—and how jealous they feel because the Tabors happen to have even more. But Nan, I believe *you* can understand that I was happier, all those years I spent here in California Gulch, taking in boarders, minding a store, and cooking meals for strangers while Horace Tabor dreamed his dreams and we struggled to get by. Now, suddenly—everything's changed. *He's* changed, so that I hardly seem to know him anymore."

That was certainly true, Nan thought. Once, Horace Tabor had been a good-natured man despite his failures—a friend to everyone, ready to grubstake a stranger with supplies from his store even though he knew there was small chance of any return. It was hard to reconcile that picture of him with the powerful mineowner stubbornly refusing to yield an inch on the miserable wages he paid the crews who dug out the silver that made him rich.

"I came over from Denver yesterday," the older woman continued, "because it had been weeks since I'd seen Horace, and there were matters that had to be discussed, face to face—mostly, about that awful house we bought that's much too big for us and that we're pouring entirely too much money into. And can you imagine the first thing I heard when I got to Leadville? A dozen people took the trouble to inform me that Horace Tabor has taken up with some woman!"

Nan suddenly felt as though a cold wind had brushed her. She made herself ask, "Can you be sure it's true?"

"Oh, it's true enough! People are always happy to let you know the worst news, with all the details. Apparently this is some blond female, hardly half his age. I haven't laid eyes on her myself, but I understand she goes by the name of Baby Doe. Can you imagine?" Augusta Tabor gave a scornful sniff. "The girls on State Street call themselves things like that! But anyway, Horace is being seen everywhere with her, including our private box at the theater. And afterward, of course, there's supper alone in that suite of his—champagne brought in and all the rest of it. Oh, and naturally I've been assured that she stays the night."

Nan hardly knew what to say or where to look. She was shocked and disappointed in her new friend, and more than a little in her own naiveté. Somehow, she had not really believed that Baby Doe could be quite so blatant and unprincipled, for all the frankness of her talk. Then Nan was suddenly struck with guilt, remembering that she had been the one to make the introduction. "What did your husband say to all this?" she asked.

"Oh, we never discussed it," Augusta said bitterly. "I found him in his office, and I took care of my business with him, and I let it go at that. Tomorrow I'm going back to Denver."

Nan saw that her hands were clutching the arms of her chair, their knuckles white.

"I suppose I'm a coward," Augusta went on, "but I tell myself it's best to hold my tongue . . . that perhaps he'll get over it on his own. It's not the first time, you know. Probably not the last, either. Horace is nearly fifty—a bad age for any man. He's going bald, he isn't young anymore, and he knows it. But of course, with all that money, there'll be women glad to play up to him and flatter him—and he may not be smart enough to know what they're after. . . ."

Driven to her feet by emotion, Augusta walked across the room to a window and stood staring into the late sunlight—a hurt and aging woman, stiff in her injured pride and disappointment. "Nan," she exclaimed, "he *needs* me! In many ways he's still a child, for all his years, and despite the luck and the money that's poured into his hands. He's throwing it all away—building opera houses, investing in projects that I don't think he really understands. Let something go wrong, and he could lose it all! We could be right back where we started—with nothing. But at least when we started we were happy. . . ."

Looking at the woman's stiffly erect figure, at the line

of her shoulders, Nan said softly, "You must love him very much."

"If I didn't," Augusta said wearily, "would I have let him bring me out from Vermont to a Kansas homestead and then across the mountains to hunt for gold he never found? Would I have borne his child, and stayed with him twenty years in this wilderness? Nan, I've *always* loved him, and I suppose I always will—though I'm beginning to wonder what good it's done either of us!"

"I'm terribly sorry!" Nan told her sincerely, but having spoken that, she could think of no other words to say.

In his short time in Leadville, Griff Cameron had become extraordinarily sensitive to the shifting moods of the boomtown. Just now, with evening settling behind a purple cloud mass that lay upon the jagged western peaks like a bruise, he had the impression that the town was marking time, waiting for something to break. There hadn't been any further eruptions coming out of the miners' strike, but as he had his supper in one of the eating houses and listened to voices around him, he had heard that one of the mines had begun barricading its shaft house—whether to protect it from rumored violence or in readiness for bringing in scab labor to man the workings, he didn't know.

On the surface things appeared calm enough, but he wondered how long such conditions could last.

Griff was in a poor mood himself after his conversation with Bill Harper. He hated having to turn down the older man's offer of a partnership. Not much of a drinking man, he nevertheless now felt the need of something to help ease the nagging tension. He walked into a crowded bar that was loud with talk, where clouds of tobacco smoke drifted below the pressed-tin ceiling. Shouldering into a place at the bar, he caught the sweating bartender's eye and signaled for a shot of whiskey. After he tasted it, he wasn't sure it was what he wanted after all, but he stood toying with the glass, frowning at his reflection in the bar mirror and only half heeding the tumble of sounds about him.

And then, reflected in the glass, a pair of eyes met his in a stare of such malevolence that it shocked him to awareness. He turned, just as Tom Riordan shoved his neighbor out of his way, clearing a space for himself at the bar. The man he displaced started to protest, saw Riordan's face, and seemed to change his mind. Riordan stared at Griff, and said roughly, "You, huh? You were supposed to have left Leadville for good."

"I don't know what gave you that idea," Griff retorted coldly. "At any rate, you can see I haven't."

It was their first encounter since their confrontation four days ago in the center of Harrison Avenue. The memory seemed to hang in the smoke-filled air as they stood at the bar, Griff with his drink forgotten on the counter at his elbow, Riordan showing a medley of stormy emotions in his heavy features. He wore a holstered gun; Griff's weapon was in his bag, on the cot in the stage-line office.

Riordan flung a challenge, his voice sharp enough to cut across the noise around them and cause talk to cease and eyes to turn on them. "What brought you to this town, anyway?"

"My own business." Griff knew it was dangerous to bait this man, but in his present mood he wasn't inclined to mince words. "Nothing to do with you."

"No?" The other's face darkened. "Damn it, you murdered one of my men!"

"If you mean Ed Luft," Griff corrected him, "that was self-defense. Ask your town marshal."

"To hell with the marshal—and to hell with Luft! I got other bones to pick, like you butting in while I was trying to deal with that Malloy bastard. Because of you, I ended up being chewed out by Morgan Slaughter—practically in front of the whole town. You got away from me that day before we could settle it!"

Griff shook his head. "You have nothing to settle with

me," he said bluntly. "You deserved whatever you got."
And in a gesture of dismissal, he turned and picked up his
unfinished drink.

That was too much for Riordan. Lashing out with a
curse, the chopping edge of his palm clipped Griff's wrist,
and the glass was torn from his fingers, leaking an amber
spray of whiskey as it hit the surface of the bar and
bounced away. Griff had no time to react; a blow of
Riordan's right fist took him on the ear and the side of the
skull, knocked his hat off, and made his whole head ring as
he stumbled into the man behind him. It was only because he caught at the edge of the bar that he didn't go
down.

Then pandemonium broke out in the excitement over
seeing a fight take shape. Men got out of the way, and
suddenly a ring had formed in the smoke-thick room. Griff
shook his head to clear it as he glanced around at the
yelling faces. And then he saw that Riordan was closing in,
not about to give his victim a chance to recover.

No expert at barroom brawling, Griff knew he would
have to move fast against Riordan, who would probably
like nothing better than to get him down and then put the
boots to him. Any mistake at such a moment could be fatal
or, at the very least, crippling. As the big fellow came at
him, Griff pushed away from the bar for momentum to
meet his rush midstride.

Riordan was wide open, his big hands reaching to
grab, when Griff went in under them. He felt a kind of
savage satisfaction as his fist took the other man just above
the belt buckle; after so much frustration, it was almost
pleasurable to feel his knuckles sink in, see this enemy
stopped in his tracks, and hear the breath gush painfully
from Riordan's suddenly gaping mouth.

Griff's head was still ringing from the first blow and
threatening to split wide open with the shouting voices
that came at him from every side. It was hard to tell which
fighter they were encouraging or whether they merely
anticipated seeing skulls broken and blood flowing, re-

gardless of whose they were. Griff braced himself. He was ready this time as Riordan, having caught his breath, gave a roar and charged him again.

They stood toe to toe, slugging it out, while the crowd went wild. The thud of blows, the scuffle of boots, and the gasps for breath were the only sounds from the fighters. No one could absorb this kind of reckless punishment for very long. Riordan's approach to fighting was spontaneous and haphazard, while Griff's chief resource was the plating of muscle and sinew that years of dealing with half-tame stage animals had formed across his arms and shoulders. He used his arms to block the bigger man's wild swings while looking for his own opportunity, and suddenly found it—Riordan missed a swing and for that moment was flung out of position, his jaw exposed.

Griff sent a blow toward the man's face, with everything he had behind it. The shock of the contact traveled up his wrist into his arm; Riordan was actually lifted off his feet and slammed sideways against the bar with an impact that rocked it, pulling its nails free from the floorboards. The big man lay crumpled at the foot of the bar, stunned but still conscious, though seeming unable to move. Griff gulped for breath as he stared down at him, only vaguely aware of the shouts of the onlookers. He knew what they expected of him—to wade in and finish this thing with his boots, while his opponent was momentarily helpless—but that was not his style.

Riordan stirred where he had fallen. He passed the back of a hand across his sweating face, looked at it as though expecting to find blood there. His eyes sought Griff's then, in a look of pure hatred. He made a convulsive, twisting movement, and his right fist came into sight from underneath his body holding the gun he had somehow managed to free from its holster.

At sight of the weapon the crowd instantly fell silent. The muzzle was aimed squarely at Griff, who could only stare at it and at the contorted face of the man who held it, certain that in another instant he would be dead. The room seemed to hold its breath.

Then someone burst through the ring of spectators and dropped upon Riordan, reaching with both hands to seize the wrist that held the gun. It was Mike Malloy, mindless of his own safety and intent on preventing a killing. Riordan tried to bring the gun onto this new target, but before he could use it, Malloy had trapped the arm, and with all his weight he twisted and wrestled it down to the sawdust-littered floor. Riordan let out a shout of rage as the gun was wrested from his hand.

He managed to wrench free of the Irishman's grasp, but the damage was done. Malloy let him go and came up to his feet holding the captured weapon. And Riordan, on his knees now, saw the muzzle of his own revolver pointed at him; it shocked sense into him. He crouched where he was, his sweating face contorted but no longer offering a fight.

Griff was stunned by the sudden turn of events. Malloy's adrenalin was up, and his brogue had never been thicker than when he told Tom Riordan, in a tone of heavy condemnation, "Sure, an' it ain't fightin' fair when you pull a gun on a man that's not wearin' one!"

In a continuing silence, Riordan reached up and hooked the edge of the bar and hauled himself to his feet. He looked around at the staring faces. He seemed suddenly aware of the serious mistake he had nearly made and of the dire result if he hadn't been stopped from shooting down an unarmed opponent in front of witnesses. He scowled but said nothing, and Malloy turned for a look at Griff. "Did he hurt you?"

"No." Griff ran a sleeve across his sweaty face. He saw his hat and bent to pick it up. "We might as well get out of here," he suggested.

"What'll I do with this?" Malloy indicated the captured weapon.

"Give it to the bartender. He can hold onto it until we're gone."

As they were leaving, the noise in the barroom quickly returned to normal. They left Tom Riordan standing alone, scowling after them and already starting to work on a stiff shot he had poured from the bar bottle. He made no move to follow them.

Outside, they found a doorway out of the flow of nighttime traffic where they could talk. Griff said, "Thanks! I almost got shot in there."

Malloy appeared sobered in the aftermath of the fight. He shook his head. "Don't even say it. I'm glad I happened to be handy. Maybe I've managed to even the score a little."

"You'll be hearing from him," Griff warned.

But the Irishman shrugged. "What's the difference? Riordan's hands have been tied, and he's only waiting for his boss to turn him loose so he can come after me. But I'll worry about that when it happens." He changed the subject. "I thought you'd left Leadville."

"I seem to be back." Briefly Griff explained the circumstances that had changed his plan, and what he was doing to help the Harper Stage Line.

"It's a worthy cause," the Irishman agreed. "Those are nice people."

"And what about your own cause?"

"The strike? You know as much as I do," Malloy said bleakly. "Except that things are simmering. Something's going to break soon; Slaughter and Tabor and them others are about to make their move—I can feel it!"

On that dark note, they parted.

Chapter Eleven

It was on the twelfth of June, a Saturday, that Nan Harper had a visitor at the stage-line office, where she sat alone, making entries into the company ledger. Something about the stranger who loomed in the open doorway— something in his hawkish features and steel-blue stare— told her this man meant trouble. She laid down her pen and asked politely, "Can I help you?"

"Maybe." He was a solid figure of a man who moved toward her with a smooth and measured stride. She was conscious of his measuring gaze. Halting before the desk, he said, "I'm Vern Showalt. I'm looking for a gent named Connors. I've come a considerable distance to find him. I'm told he may work for this outfit."

She shook her head. "No, I'm sorry. I'm afraid you've been misinformed. I don't know anyone by the name of Connors."

Not answering, the man took a square of stiff cardboard from his coat pocket and laid it on the desk. Nan stared at it and felt a sudden coldness somewhere inside her. She was looking at a photograph of a stagecoach and six-horse team standing before a station, with the legend MONTANA STAGES painted over its door; the coach seemed ready to roll. In the windows were passengers, and yard hands stood about, along with a clerk in an eyeshade and sleeve protectors. Vern Showalt laid a blunt forefinger on the figure of the driver, seated on the box with the ribbons gathered in his hands, waiting for the photographer to finish his work.

"That's the man," Showalt said. "Griff Connors—though I understand he's been calling himself Cameron hereabouts; odd that he wouldn't bother to change his *first* name. I've asked around, since I arrived, and I've been told that he drives stages for your company. Isn't that true?"

For a moment Nan could not find her voice; it was almost too great an effort even to breathe. Though the man on the driver's seat in the photograph wore a dark mustache, there was no chance of mistaking the identity of Griff Cameron.

She cleared her throat. Trying to gain time for her thoughts to settle, she said bluntly, "You haven't told me yet who *you* are, Mr. Showalt—or why you happen to be interested in this man."

Showalt lifted a shoulder. "Very well. Skipping the details, I'm an express company detective, investigating a recent stage holdup in Montana. The guard was murdered, and a considerable shipment of money was stolen. Griff Connors drove the stage and served the highwaymen as their tipoff." He went on after a moment, reading the expression on her face. "You appear to doubt what I'm telling you. It happens to be fact. I had my hands on Connors, but he got away. I've followed him here, clear to Leadville—and I can tell you I don't mean to leave without him!"

Nan sat stunned, absorbing this. All too well she could remember feeling that there was some secret surrounding the man she knew as Griff Cameron—and there had been his mysterious warning on the day he went to work for the stage line: *There are reasons why I might have to pick up and go, almost at a moment's notice. . . .* From the moment she first knew him, she had been conscious of a shadow hanging over the man. Now, at last, she understood what that shadow was.

But she also knew, somehow, that a dreadful mistake had been made. And guilty or not, she couldn't turn against someone who had come to earn her gratitude and trust. Her decision made, she told Showalt, "I'm afraid you're too late. Mr. Cameron—Connors—is no longer here. He's gone."

"Oh?" The man stiffened slightly; his pale stare narrowed. "Gone where?"

"He never said. He drew his pay and just said he was leaving Leadville. That was yesterday morning. . . ."

The detective continued to stare at her. Knowing herself to be an inexpert liar, she felt her cheeks grow warm, but she stood her ground, hardly even caring now if he believed her. She was sure there was a glint of cold mockery in his pale eyes as he nodded curtly and said, "Well, in that case, I'm sorry for having bothered you. Good day." He picked up the photograph and returned it to his pocket. With no further words, he turned his back and walked away from her and out of the stage-line office.

Nan sat for a long moment, fighting to control her breathing and anguished emotion. With a sudden urgency she got to her feet and crossed to the doorway. She stopped short when she saw Showalt and Dick Walsh standing together in the sun, talking. A hand lifted to her throat, she watched anxiously, dreading to think what they might be saying. She expected to see the photograph brought out again. Instead, the stranger seemed to be asking questions; now he nodded, as though satisfied with the answers, and turning, walked briskly toward the gate.

Nan waited until he was gone; then she left her post and hurried into the yard. Dick had started toward the barn; he came back as she called to him.

"That man who just left," she exclaimed. "What was he talking to you about?"

Something in her manner caused the youth to stammer a little. "Why, n-nothing much. He was looking for

Mr. Cameron—told me he was an old friend who wanted to see him. So I just said Griff had walked over across town a little while ago. There seems to be something going on that could be connected with the strike, and he wanted to look into it. So the man said he'd go look around, maybe run into him. . . . Why?" he added hastily, seeing the look on her face. "What's the matter? Did I say something I shouldn't?"

Nan bit her lip in keen anxiety. Not answering, she made a sudden decision. "Quick!" She seized the startled youngster by an arm. "I need your help with the buggy. . . ."

Working with such haste that the bay horse grew upset, they got him between the shafts and in record time had the harness on him. Dick asked no more questions when he saw Nan was not going to answer them. She got into the rig, took the reins in one hand and the whip in the other, and spoke to the old horse in a tone that got him moving out of the yard at a brisk pace.

Nan turned her buggy in the direction of Harrison Avenue, acutely aware that she had no real idea where to find Griff. There did indeed seem to be something afoot in Leadville, she soon realized. The steady thump of a drum, like a pulse beat, had begun to sound across the stillness, and as though drawn to it, men were hurrying along the paths and wooden sidewalks, running or walking fast toward the heart of town. She heard excited yells and wondered if the whole place had gone crazy.

She felt almost certain of it a moment later when, without warning, a pair of men darted into the street and came directly toward her. One seemed intent on grabbing the headstall of the bay, the second leaped for the iron step of the buggy itself. Nan saw a tough and unshaven face, the mouth open in a shout, as the man reached for her. Too angry to be frightened, she raised the whip and lashed at him. She felt the whip connect, and the man's shout turned into a yell of pain. He lost his unsure footing and fell back, arms flailing as he dropped out of sight into the street dust.

The second man was having no better luck. The nervous bay, upset enough as it was, had reacted with panic to someone dashing wildly toward it. It pulled away from the grasping fingers and tried to rear. Nan thought for an instant the rig was going to jackknife and spill there in the middle of the street. She called to the horse and touched it with the whip, settling the animal enough so that it dropped to all four hooves and leaped ahead, the buggy straightening with a jerk. The second man had to scramble backward to avoid being run down. She caught no more than a glimpse of his face as she spun past and left him standing.

It happened all too swiftly for her to imagine what the pair of men had wanted. Putting it down to the insanity that seemed to have infected all of Leadville today, she quickly forgot them as she arrived at the intersection with Harrison Avenue. There she reined in the bay and stared about in frowning puzzlement.

Leadville's principal thoroughfare was normally a busy place early on a Saturday afternoon, but today it seemed at first glance to lie completely empty. Immediately Nan realized her mistake: As she looked down the street, she saw that the boardwalk on either side of the empty thoroughfare was jammed with people—standing silent, motionless in expectant waiting.

And then a bass drum sounded—so loud and close at hand that her head jerked about with a start.

Four abreast, resplendent in scarlet uniforms with gold braid, their rifle barrels gleaming at shoulder arms, a group of men came marching toward her down the center of the avenue. A stern-looking figure on horseback preceded them, and after him came the bass drum, its solid beat setting the pace, sending echoes reverberating from building fronts. The nervous buggy horse laid back its ears and tried to move about between the shafts. Nan spoke to the animal to settle it, as she wondered just what was happening.

Then, among the men who lined the opposite side of

the street, she saw a face she recognized. She estimated
the distance of the marching column, deciding she had
just enough time to get across before it reached her, and
impulsively slapped the reins against the bay's rump. Un-
willingly, the horse moved forward into the intersection.
The buggy cleared the street with time to spare, and
pulling up at the corner, Nan called to Mike Malloy.

Despite the drum and ragged tramp of boots, he
heard her cry and came to her. Leaning, she asked, "Mike,
what in the world is it—a parade? Who are those men?"

Mike Malloy's broad Irish face showed bitterness.
"Ain't they a handsome lot?" he said with heavy sarcasm.
"Those fine lads are the Tabor Guard."

"But I don't understand!" She looked again at the
marching men, at the shining rifles held awkwardly at
their shoulders. "I've never seen them armed."

"I guess you ain't heard about what's going on," he
suggested bleakly.

The expression on his face alarmed her. "I've been
keeping pretty much to myself," she admitted. "I haven't
heard anything."

He raised his voice above the thunder of the nearing
drum. "Horace Tabor wired the governor that the strike
was getting out of hand, turning violent—not a word of it
true, of course! But he said he needed help keeping order.
And now," he went on loudly, "Governor Pitkin has gone
and sent a wagonload of guns and ammunition—enough
for a regiment. He's given the okay for Tabor to turn his
guard into militia and then go ahead and recruit as many
more as he wants! And here's the result. Would you just
look at 'em!"

They all but filled the street, marching behind their
mounted leader. Nan recognized him now; he was Colonel
Bohn, a spare and bearded businessman and Civil War
veteran, wearing his faded uniform and sitting the saddle
like General Grant himself, with sunlight glinting from the
blade of a brandished sword. But what alarmed her more
than the aging colonel or the guard itself were the men

who followed after them—a lot of men, not in uniform, who shuffled through the street dust without much discipline and scarcely bothering to keep in step. These, then, were Tabor's newly recruited "militia." Some were probably Leadville citizens, stirred to answer the call and save their community from threatened danger; but many more were of a different sort entirely, hardened and tough, and all too familiar with the weapons they carried.

She heard Malloy's dark comment: "You see 'em too, lass? Those are the ones the owners hired and brought in for strikebreakers—only now they got the official backing of the state of Colorado behind them. From here on, any damn thing they take it in their heads to do to us is all right! And if *they* can't finish us off, I understand the governor's already promised to send in state troops and declare martial law. And that will be the beginning of the end." Malloy shook his head, scowling bleakly. "Tabor and his friends are paradin' the militia in front of us 'cause they figure they got us licked. An' I can't see but what they're right!"

It was no wonder, then, that the strikers and their sympathizers, standing along the sidewalks, watched in utter silence as this armed force paraded its strength. There were no catcalls, no demonstrations—only a stillness, dominated by the tramp of boots and the steady beat of the drum. Nan's sympathies were with the miners, but she had her own urgent concern, which made her say now to Malloy, "Mike, I'm looking for Griff Cameron. It's very important. I was wondering if by any chance you might have seen him."

"Cameron? I was talking to him, right on this spot—not more'n twenty minutes ago."

"I've got to find him!" she insisted. "Did you notice where he went?"

"Why, on down the street. He may be somewhere down that way if I ain't mistaken." He gestured toward the lower end of Harrison. The Irishman added quickly, "But you'd never get through now."

She saw he was right; the marchers blocked the avenue to any other traffic. Nan hesitated only briefly. She lifted the reins as she thanked Malloy with a nod. "That's all right," she said. "I can go around. . . ."

She flicked the reins and sent the bay horse on to the next corner, where she turned south on Pine. The back streets paralleling Harrison were virtually deserted just now, the whole town being drawn to the sound of the drum beat and the spectacle of armed men parading through Leadville like an occupying force. At each crossing she glanced over toward the avenue, saw more crowds blocking it, and went on without pause. But finally, reaching State Street, Harrison looked clear, and she swung again in that direction.

Nan, well aware of State's unsavory reputation, had always been careful to avoid it, but today she scarcely noticed the tawdry dives that crowded its length. She got out near the intersection with Harrison, tied the bay's reins, and continued afoot, with no more than a glance at a derelict slumped soddenly in a doorway who leered after her as she hurried off.

When she came out on Harrison, she found she had indeed bypassed the crowd, which appeared to have gathered in front of the Clarendon Hotel and the Opera House. She started in that direction, lifting her skirt above the thick dust of the unpaved street. But as she neared the crowd, she began to realize how slim her chances were of picking out one face among this confused mass. And even if Griff Cameron was here and she did see him, to get close enough to warn him about the man who called himself Vern Showalt would be still another matter.

She gained the edge of the crowd, which blocked the street in front of the Clarendon. For once her height was an advantage as she stood on tiptoe for a clearer view.

The parading militia appeared to have reached their destination—the Tabor Opera House. Nan saw that a window of Horace Tabor's second-floor suite had been opened, allowing him and Morgan Slaughter to climb out onto a balcony just above the building's central doorway. From there they could look down upon the ranks of armed men and onlookers in the street below. Now the drum fell silent. In the resulting stillness a confused shuffling of feet could be heard as the last stragglers came filing up into position and halted. Sunlight flashed on the steel blade as Colonel Bohn raised his sword, gave a brisk military salute to Horace Tabor, and then reined aside.

One man in the crowd apparently could hold himself back no longer. Not far from Nan, he shouted something at the colonel—she could not make out exactly what it was, but the self-important leader of the militia heard and stiffened. Dignity suddenly forgotten, he jerked his head around and called out furiously, "Who said that?" He must have thought he had spotted the heckler, for without waiting for an answer, he gave a kick that sent his horse charging straight at the crowd, and his dress sword was raised to strike.

Stumbling over one another, men gave way before the lunging animal. Nan saw that she was in danger and turned to escape, but at that moment someone collided with her and she was knocked from her feet. Sprawling in the street dust, she heard the yells all about her and felt the reverberations of a horse's hooves striking the ground, but she was too confused to know what to do.

A familiar voice called her name, and then a hand seized her arm and pulled her up to her feet, out of danger. She looked into the anxious face of Baby Doe, who said, "Are you all right?"

Nan nodded, catching her breath. She looked about then and saw Colonel Bohn. He had found his heckler and, holding the nervous horse on a tight rein so that it pranced around under him, leaned from the saddle, yelling furiously as he struck at the man with the flat of his sword. The fellow's hat went flying; he wrapped his arms protectively around his head as he twisted and tried to evade the blows.

But now Nan saw someone come running up—it was

the town marshal, Jud Osland. Without hesitation, he closed in, reached and seized the horseman, and simply dumped him from the saddle. Colonel Bohn lost his sword; his victim went reeling away. Osland dragged the colonel to his feet, shouting angrily, "What do you think you're doing? Are you *trying* to start a riot?"

The colonel, dignity ruffled and uniform badly disarrayed, sputtered in protest. Disgustedly, the lawman cut him off. "Me and my deputies are trying not to let this foolishness end in bloodshed. Looks like I'll have to put you someplace where you can't make things any worse." He signaled to a policeman, who came hurrying. Osland shoved the colonel into his hands. "Take him and lock him up where he can cool off. The charge is disturbing the peace."

Bohn was led away, arguing furiously, while a few onlookers cheered. Nan was still a little dazed by events, but she had a feeling the marshal's quick action might have prevented a disaster. As it was, the incident seemed to have passed without much notice. Up there on the balcony of the Opera House, Morgan Slaughter was now speaking to the crowd, and they had quieted to listen; his voice sounded thin in the stillness.

Baby Doe was still at Nan's side. "I thought I was going to see you trampled, right there in front of me!" she exclaimed. "You sure you're all right?"

"I'm fine," Nan insisted. She pushed at her tangled hair, trying absently to put it into some kind of shape.

Her friend said urgently, "We better get out of this street before something worse happens."

Nan shook her head. "I can't. I'm looking for someone, but I don't see him."

"And you won't—not in *this* crazy mob!" Baby Doe tugged at her hand. "Come with me. I'll take you where you can get a much better view."

Before Nan could protest, she was being hauled away, straight toward the entrance of the Clarendon. A clot of bystanders watching in the doorway separated to let them enter. Baby Doe made her way across the elegant lobby, with its deep-napped carpet, tall mirrors, and well-upholstered furniture, and took the broad stairs to the second floor and then to the third, with Nan firmly in tow.

She seemed to know exactly where she was going. She led her friend along a hallway past a double row of closed doors, and at one of these she halted. The door, left unlocked, opened when she turned the knob, and she ushered the other woman inside.

Nan halted on the threshold. "Who do you know that lives in a place like *this*?"

"Me!" Baby Doe closed the door and crossed quickly to an open window, but for a moment Nan could only stand and stare at the hotel room and its furnishings.

Actually it was part of a suite, for she could see the bedroom through a door that stood ajar. She had heard rumors of the Clarendon's elegance, but she hadn't been prepared for the marble-topped tables, the gilt chairs worked in needlepoint, the chaise longue, the valanced window drapes, and the painted vase that held a peacock feather—all in the latest 1880 style. Not two weeks ago, she had settled Baby Doe into a single room in a modest Leadville boardinghouse; looking around her now, she wondered at her friend's change of domicile . . . until she noticed a photograph in a silver frame, prominently displayed on the center table.

It was a photograph of Horace Tabor. All at once Nan remembered her visit with Augusta, and the woman's bitter comments. She understood everything, and her heart sank.

Baby Doe was at the window, gesturing impatiently. "Come here!" Not sure how she could be friendly or even casual with the blond woman after what she now knew or suspected, Nan reluctantly went to join her.

The suite overlooked Harrison Avenue, three stories below. By leaning a little from the window, Nan and Baby Doe could glimpse the facade of the Opera House next door, and the balcony where Tabor and Slaughter still stood.

By now Slaughter had finished haranguing the crowd, and it was Tabor's turn. The crowd heard him in sullen silence as he told of his efforts to treat the striking miners fairly, until they had made it impossible. Finally, his hand having been forced, he had moved judiciously and with timely speed to prevent the situation from breaking down in mob violence—something he would never allow in Leadville. As he talked on and on in this vein, Nan suddenly inhaled sharply, but then shook her head to the question in Baby Doe's glance.

"I guess I was mistaken. I thought for a moment I saw Griff Cameron down there."

"Cameron?" Baby Doe thought a moment. "The man who got us past the rock slide that day? Is he the one you're so concerned about?"

"I have an important message for him. If I could just find him—"

She broke off at the startling report of a rifle shot.

It was impossible to locate its origin, but they saw Horace Tabor suddenly drop from sight behind the balcony rail above the doorway of the Opera House. Nan heard a choked gasp of horror from her companion and turned to see Baby Doe's face white with shock. The blond woman's mouth worked soundlessly, and then the words came: "Oh, he's dead! He's *dead!*"

Nan caught her by the shoulder, but Baby Doe wrenched free. She was already turning away, heedless when Nan called after her to wait. Baby Doe reached the door, flung it open, and vanished. With no more than a moment's hesitation, Nan went after her, all disapproval forgotten in her sympathy for her friend's distress.

She knew where Baby Doe was headed. At the far end of the corridor, she saw a flight of steps, which could only lead to the walkway connecting the upper stories of the Clarendon and the Opera House next door. Baby Doe was hurriedly climbing them; by the time Nan reached the stairs, her friend's footsteps were already sounding in the walkway, which hung suspended above the alley three stories below.

It turned out to be a narrow, roofed passageway, with a skylight and a couple of gas jets for illumination. At its other end she found more steps, which led down to the second floor of the Opera House. Baby Doe was still somewhere ahead, for the light click of heels could be heard; she was moving with the assurance of one who had taken this route often enough to know her way. Nan followed the footsteps, and so came to a part of the building that she recognized—a carpeted hallway, with the balcony entrance on one side and the door to Horace Tabor's private quarters on the other.

That door had been closed the few times she and her grandfather had seen it. Now it stood wide open. Approaching hesitantly, Nan peered into the inner sanctum of the silver king of Leadville.

She saw Baby Doe standing in the center of a big and richly furnished room. Yonder, through a second door, she could glimpse the open window to the balcony above the street. Even as she watched, Horace Tabor crawled awkwardly in through the window, with Morgan Slaughter close behind him. Tabor was standing, brushing and straightening his clothing, when he noticed Baby Doe. He exclaimed, "Baby! You look like you'd seen a ghost!"

She rushed forward then and threw her arms around him. "You aren't hurt?" she cried. "We heard the gun go off—and I saw you fall! Oh, I thought sure—"

"Hell, he missed by a mile," Tabor assured her, taking her into his embrace. "Never even busted a window. But I'm no fool—I wasn't gonna just stand there while somebody used me for a target. I ducked for cover!"

With her cheek pressed against his chest, Baby Doe's voice was muffled in the aftermath of terror. "I was so *scared!*"

Watching this scene, Nan was struck with the thought: *Why, she really does care about him!* It might have been

Horace Tabor's wealth that first attracted Baby Doe; perhaps she'd even cold-bloodedly set her cap for him, despite his being married. But in this moment Nan felt
certain her friend's behavior was that of a woman sincerely
in love and terrified for the safety of her man. Moreover,
there was a surprising gentleness in the way Horace Tabor
held her to him.

Now, as Tabor looked at Nan above Baby Doe's golden
curls, Nan blurted out, to cover her own confusion, "Who
fired the shot?"

Horace Tabor shook his head. "I have no idea. It
came from a window across the street. Had to be one of
that scum, of course," he went on, his anger returning.
He released Baby Doe from his arms. "Like I told them
out there, I've tried to be reasonable, but I don't have to
put up with *this*! The governor's goin' to get a wire this
very day, calling on him to help settle things by sendin'
troops and declarin' martial law, like he promised me!"

"The sooner the better," Slaughter agreed crisply. He
pushed by Tabor and came to Nan, exclaiming, "But what
in the world has happened to *you*?"

She realized he was staring at her dust-streaked and
rumpled clothing. Looking down at herself, she said, "It
was nothing, really. Down in front of the hotel, a few
minutes ago, I got bumped into and lost my footing."

"You should never have been there! Not with all
that's going on. My God, you could have been seriously
injured!" Slaughter laid a hand possessively on her shoulder. "Give me another moment or two with Horace, and
then I want to see that you get home safe."

"That really isn't necessary," she insisted, moving
from under the weight of his hand. "I left my horse and
rig close by. I can manage. I don't intend to let anything
happen to me."

"Well . . ." He must have seen she was not to be
persuaded; he shrugged, frowning. "I won't argue about
it. But promise me you'll be careful."

"Of course." She hadn't forgotten the purpose that

brought her across town in the first place, and at an opportune moment she excused herself.

She hurried through the silent theater, passed the double doors of the auditorium, and descended the grand staircase to the lobby. Out on the street she found the area in front of the Opera House mostly cleared; the Tabor Guard and the militia had apparently been marched away, and the crowd of onlookers was gradually dispersing. But when she searched anxiously for any glimpse of Griff Cameron, she was disappointed. Plainly, she would have to begin her quest all over again.

But first she had to reclaim her horse and buggy from where she had left them on State Street. She found them intact. She was just reaching for the reins, prior to climbing into the buggy, when two men came at her.

They were on her almost before she knew it. A hand fastened upon her arm. She jerked free, turning, and looked into a face that bore the mark of a buggy whip— from that earlier attack when she was leaving the stage yard. She was too angry to wonder what the pair meant to do, or even to be frightened. She struck out, and her fist scraped beard stubble. The man swore at her, and she caught the reek of whiskey on his breath.

Then a hand cuffed her on the side of the head, a blow that dazed her and filled her vision with stars. Her knees sagged. Dimly, she was aware that the pair crowded in to seize and hold her upright. After that, she was scarcely aware of anything.

Chapter Twelve

In the two hours after the explosive events he'd witnessed on Harrison Avenue, Griff Cameron saw a change in Leadville. He could feel its mood in the silences, in the despairing voices he heard around him after that naked display of force by the mineowners. Not seeing Mike Malloy or Frank Gower, he had no one to discuss the situation with, but he had no doubt what they would have told him.

Things had taken a disastrous turn. Up to this point matters had hung in the air, the strike dragging on inconclusively; but now that was sure to change. His friends had taken on too powerful an adversary. As soon as the owners decided to bring the full weight of their money and their political strength to bear, things were bound to come to a showdown.

He heard someone remark bitterly, "We never had a chance, going easy with the likes of Morgan Slaughter. We should have taken off our gloves and really fought 'em—busted things up some, instead of trying to make the bastards admit we had right on our side! That might have got us somewhere!" Well, perhaps, but Griff began to wonder if their cause hadn't been doomed from the start.

Then something happened, and suddenly all concern for other people's problems was wiped from Griff's mind.

He was standing in a doorway, out of the stream of traffic, preparing to put a match to a cigar, his after-supper indulgence. The long day was dying behind the black rim of mountains to the west. The gas lamps along Harrison Avenue were being lit, one by one, but this end of the street was still bathed in grainy twilight. When the man passed him, Griff saw his face for only an instant in the glow from a lighted window. And he froze, grateful at that moment for his shadowed doorway, for his pulled-down hat brim, and for the hands cupped about the unlighted cigar shielding his face.

When the man was gone, Griff was left with a sharply etched impression of hawkish features, a jutting nose, a strong jaw, and hollowed eyes. He slipped the cigar unlit back into his pocket and stepped out from the doorway, looking after the figure quickly being swallowed by the dusk. Ever since his fight in the bar with Tom Riordan, Griff had taken the precaution of wearing his gun and holster in this town. Now, half consciously, he laid a hand on the butt of the Smith and Wesson.

At first he had had no doubt that the man he'd seen was Vern Showalt. But almost at once, he began to question his first impression. Certain that the express company detective couldn't be far behind him, it was only natural for his imagination to work on a general resemblance and turn it into the face of his pursuer. But even as he told himself this, a nagging voice said there had been no mistake; that man had looked too much like Showalt for Griff to ignore.

Supposing it was only a case of nerves and his imagination had been overactive—still, he told himself as he stood there, it was high time for him to be moving on. There was no reason for him to stay, after all. The emergency that had threatened the Harper Stage Line had passed; Jerry was recovered enough from his injuries that in a day or two he would be able to take his place again on the box of a stagecoach. Griff had stretched his luck, remaining this long. He had to start thinking about himself.

But even as he started walking toward the Harper place, he knew saying good-bye wouldn't be easy. For him to leave now, practically without warning, would go hard with Nan's grandfather—a blow the old man probably couldn't be made to understand. Griff had tried to prepare Nan for it as best he could without explaining his reasons; he knew that she would accept his decision and not ask unanswerable questions. Even so, he was forced to admit that saying good-bye to her was going to be the hardest part of all.

In a few short weeks, something about that woman—her honesty, her directness of manner—had made a strong impression on him, a greater impact than from any other woman he could recall. And that was all the more reason, he saw now with harsh clarity, why he was going to have to make a clean break: The trail ahead allowed no place for a relationship.

So he felt urgency and reluctance, too, as he went through the gate in the picket fence and up the path to the house where Nan and her grandfather lived. It was fully dark now, and lamplight showed in the windows. He paused for a moment with arm raised to knock, hating to do this. But it could not be put off. Griff knocked and waited—but only briefly, for almost at once the door was jerked open. Bill Harper stared out at him.

The old man looked wild, and with a strange pallor. "Griff!" he exclaimed, before the visitor could speak. "Do you know anything?"

Puzzled, Griff said, "About what?"

"Why . . . Nan, of course!"

The older man's appearance and the tone of his voice caused a cold knot of apprehension to tighten in Griff's chest. Quickly, he stepped through the door to confront Bill Harper. "Is something wrong with Nan?"

Animation died in the old man's face. His shoulders

sagged and he grunted, "I guess you haven't heard. . . . Griff, they've got her!"

"Who has?" Griff snapped. "For God's sake, what are you talking about?" When Bill merely looked at him, eyes distraught in an ashen face, he took the old man by an elbow and steered him to a horsehair sofa. He forced him to sit there and took his place beside him. "Now!" he ordered. "Tell me everything—from the beginning!"

Bill's mouth trembled, but he got it out. "I've just been to Horace Tabor's office. He and Slaughter and the marshal were there. They had a letter . . . and a ring. They wanted to know if it belonged to Nan."

"Did it?"

The old fellow nodded, miserably. "It was her Grandma's. Just a cheap ring, but Nan loved to wear it."

Griff Cameron thought he remembered seeing it on her finger—a simple golden band, with a tiny stone of some sort. "All right," he said grimly. "Now what's this about a letter?"

"The marshal showed it to me. It wasn't even signed. Looked almost like some little kid's printing, but they told me that it was done deliberatly to disguise the handwriting. Griff, the thing was a ransom note! It said they were holding Nan, and they sent along the ring to prove it. Said she wouldn't be hurt—unless they didn't get what they wanted." He choked off.

"I don't understand. With this stage line in the shape it's in, just what kind of a ransom does anyone think you'd be in a position to pay?"

Bill shook his head. "Morgan insists the thing is aimed squarely at him. And I guess, at that, he ain't made any secret of the way he feels about that girl. The whole town knows he'd like to marry her, only for some reason she ain't been willing to give him the least encouragement. Anyhow, the letter says that unless him and the other owners agree to give the strikers what they been asking for—and fork over fifty thousand in cash by midnight—

then none of us will ever see Nan alive again!" The old man's hands knotted together, trembling.

Griff repeated the amount in disbelief. "Even Slaughter couldn't be expected to have that kind of money lying around, ready to lay his hands on at a moment's notice!"

"That's what *he* said! But he blames himself—he swore that he'd work this out one way or another and see to it Nan didn't end up getting hurt."

"How the hell can he make that kind of promise?"

The old man shook his head in despair. "I don't know either. They were talking it over when I left, not getting anywhere that I could see. I came on home, and I been sitting here waiting. Griff, I don't know what to *do*!"

"There's nothing right now you *can* do," Griff said gently. He placed a hand on Bill's arm and felt the tenseness in the stringy muscles. "You stay put. And try not to worry—it doesn't do any good. I'll try to find out what's going on, maybe see if I can have a word with that marshal. He's a good man, and he may have some ideas. If I learn anything at all, I promise I'll keep you posted."

Nan's grandfather nodded, begging him with frightened eyes. "You do that, Griff. Please!"

It was only afterward, as he was hurrying toward the marshal's office, that Griff realized he had forgotten everything else, including the man who might or might not be his enemy from the express company. All at once, even Vern Showalt didn't seem important. Bill Harper's news had filled him with anger, and with something else—an understanding, born of Nan's predicament, of just how much that woman had come to matter to him.

Did it really mean he was in love with her? Griff faced the question for the first time . . . and was afraid he knew the answer.

He hardly knew what he expected to discover at the jail—perhaps nothing at all, or a bored deputy holding down the desk while his boss was out of the office somewhere. But as he approached he could hear angry voices, audible even though the jail building's door and windows were all fast shut. Griff turned the knob and stepped inside.

No one appeared to notice him, and he quietly closed the door and put his back to it. Two men stood before the marshal's desk in heated confrontation. They were Mike Malloy and Morgan Slaughter; lamplight showed the angry faces of these two leaders on opposite sides of the miners' strike that had paralyzed Leadville. Behind the desk, sunk deep in his chair, Marshal Osland watched them with no expression on his face, but with a keen-eyed stare that shuttled from one man to the other as they exchanged hostile words.

Slaughter was speaking. He pointed a stabbing forefinger at Malloy as he demanded harshly, "I'd like to know how long you mean to stand there denying what we all know damn well to be true!"

"I can't help what you think might be true," the Irishman retorted. "What I'm telling you is fact!"

"And I say you're lying!" Slaughter swung around to the seated marshal. "Now that you got him, I'm holding you responsible that he doesn't walk out of here before Nan Harper is set safely free!"

Hands laced across his middle, the lawman spoke calmly. "Malloy ain't under arrest. He came in of his own accord, to tell what he knows about Nan and the ransom letter—which seems to be nothing at all."

"And you believe him?" Slaughter retorted. "Hell, he's been one of the masterminds of this strike from the beginning. Now that the governor's stepping in, and things have turned against them, he and his friends are ready to try anything—including kidnapping and attempted murder and who knows what else!"

Malloy's brogue thickened as his temper flared. "Sure, an' I don't have to take this! None of my people know who fired that shot at you and Tabor today. And for a fact, none of us would dream of doin' mischief to a fine lass like Nan Harper. That letter was *none* of our doin'."

"Then why does it say—?"

Griff cut the man off in midsentence. "Anybody can write an unsigned ransom note, Slaughter. They can make any kind of demands . . . and throw suspicion on anyone they like. But you'd best figure all they're really interested in is the money."

The mineowner's head whipped around; his eyes met Griff's in a malevolent stare. "Who the hell asked for *your* opinion?"

"He makes sense," the marshal said, in the same mild tone as before. "I agree with him. I can't arrest Malloy or anyone else on no better evidence than an unsigned letter."

"No?" Crossed at every side, Slaughter demanded sharply, "You want to keep your job?"

"Not that bad!" The marshal was on his feet suddenly, facing the mineowner across the littered desk. "Morgan, I'm doing all I can. I've got my own men out, and some of Tabor's militia, tracking down every possible clue. So far we've come up with nothing. If you want me fired, I guess you've got the power to do it—so go right ahead. But while I have this job, I'm telling you to keep hands off and let me do it according to my own rights! You understand?"

Slaughter's chest swelled; he seemed about to explode in further strong language, but Osland merely waited, giving him back the stubborn resistance of a man sure of his own values. Slaughter must have sensed that verbal abuse would not sway him, for he made an angry grimace, swung his shoulders, and turned away without so much as another glance at Mike Malloy.

But he had a last antagonistic stare for Griff as the latter stepped calmly aside, out of his way. Their eyes met for a long moment. Then Slaughter wrenched open the door and slammed through it, his bootheels echoing as he strode away.

"The son of a bitch!" Griff muttered.

But the marshal spoke without heat. "You got to consider what this thing has done to him, Cameron. Maybe you hadn't realized that he's been almighty interested in that girl. Been after her to marry him, but without getting anywhere, I guess."

"Yeah, I know about that," Griff answered shortly.

"So did the kidnappers, apparently. Slaughter figures the ransom demand is aimed squarely at him. And he's already made up his mind that he's got no choice but to pay."

"By himself? The whole fifty thousand?"

The lawman nodded. "Exactly—rather than risk harm being done to the girl. I was there in Tabor's office when the two of them settled on a deal."

"What kind of a deal?"

"Tabor is assuming the title to Slaughter's Horseshoe mine, at not much more than half what it's worth. Those were the best terms he'd offer, and Morgan had to accept. After all, the ransom has to be in cash, and Tabor is going to have to do some scrounging around and sell off some properties in order to raise it." The lawman perched on the side of the desk. "He's working at that right now, and he's promised to have the cash ready in a couple of hours. So you see, Morgan Slaughter has good reason to act edgy. He may be a tough man, but what he's doing can't leave much doubt how concerned he is for Nan Harper."

Malloy shook his head in wonder. "I never would have thought it of him."

Griff Cameron, for his part, was silenced; the extent of Slaughter's sacrifice stunned him. *A strange man, no two ways about it!* Griff found himself wondering if, perhaps, Slaughter had some notion his gesture would change Nan's unyielding attitude toward him, even win her over. . . .

Malloy asked the marshal, "You want anything more with me? Or can I go?"

A gesture from Osland dismissed him. The lawman asked Griff, "Have you seen Bill Harper?"

He nodded. "He gave me the news of what had happened to his granddaughter."

"How's he seem to be taking it?"

"Pretty hard, I'm afraid."

The marshal shook his head in sympathy. "Let him know I'm doing everything I can—which ain't much, so far. Even if they're holding her in town, there's no telling where it might be in a place the size of Leadville. The last thing I want to have to do is mount a house-to-house search. No telling where that would end!"

Afterward, in the darkness outside the office, Griff and Malloy stood unspeaking, each busy with his own thoughts and listening to the sounds of Leadville on a Saturday night. It was Malloy who remarked suddenly, "I guess I haven't mentioned it, but I saw Nan today. It couldn't have been very long before she was snatched. She was trying to find you."

"Me?" Griff echoed quickly.

"And mightily worked up about it, too. It was during all that commotion on the avenue. She was alone, driving a buggy. I told her I'd seen you heading down toward the Opera House, but it didn't seem like she'd be able to get through, so she said she'd try to find another way. Did she locate you?"

"No." Griff was all the more baffled and concerned, trying to imagine what could have sent Nan searching for him.

Malloy went on, "I understand she made it to the Opera House—Slaughter saw her there. But after that, nobody seems to know anything. Damn!" the Irishman exploded. "Aside from her being too nice a person for this to happen to, it does look like somebody is out to lay it onto my friends and me! I got plenty reason for wantin' to get to the bottom of this, just as bad as anybody. . . ."

With no real aim in mind, they left the jail and put their backs to the gulch, starting up the broad length of Harrison Avenue, each silent in his dark thoughts. They had crossed State Street and passed a few steps farther when suddenly Griff halted, belatedly realizing what he had just seen. "Wait a minute!" Griff turned back, and Malloy followed him around the corner onto State.

There, almost lost in shadow, a top buggy stood with a bay horse droop-headed between its shafts. As Malloy joined him Griff said curtly, "This is Nan's rig!"

The Irishman nodded. "It looks like the one I saw her driving. She must have left it here and gone to the Opera House afoot."

"And never came back," Griff added. "On State Street, the wonder is somebody didn't help himself to an abandoned rig, make off with it. . . ."

A voice said, "You gents be lookin' for a lady?"

They both turned. They hadn't noticed the man before—he was sprawled in a darkened doorway, only his face palely visible. The reek of cheap whiskey came from him, and Malloy said curtly, "We're damn well lookin' for a lady!"

The fellow appeared to try to get on his feet, but he gave it up and dropped soddenly back. His voice was so thick it was almost incoherent as he insisted, "I was sittin' right here. I seen her drive up and get out and walk away." He made a vague gesture in the direction of Harrison.

Griff impatiently cut him off. "We know that already." He motioned for Malloy to climb into the buggy and then reached for the reins.

"After while," the drunk went on, as though he hadn't heard, "the lady come back. . . ."

It took Griff an instant for this to soak in. He whirled on the man in the doorway. *"What did you say?"*

The man cringed away from him. "I didn't do nothin'!" he cried in a frightened whine. "It was them others!"

"What others?" Griff caught the man by his clothing, half raised and thrust the drunk, hard, against the jamb of the door. "Look here! If you know something, you'd better tell it—*fast!*"

"I'm *tellin'* you!" the derelict babbled, frantically. "There was two of 'em. They showed up and I seen 'em hanging around and keeping an eye on the rig—kind of like waiting. And when she come back and started to get in, they jumped her and dragged her off. I dunno where."

"And nobody tried to stop them?" Griff demanded harshly.

"Wasn't nobody. Only me—and I couldn't do nothin'!" the man insisted, writhing in his grasp. "I—I was *sick!*"

Griff shook the derelict and said harshly, "What did they look like? *Tell me!*"

"I—I don't rightly know 'cause they ran off so fast, and like I said, I was sick, and . . ."

Suddenly he was crying. Griff, aware of the sour odor of whiskey on his clothing, could well believe the man had been sick. He dumped him back in his place, fished a silver dollar from his pocket, and dropped it in the derelict's lap with a curt, "Thanks."

Malloy, who had heard the entire exchange, clutched Griff's arm. "What do you think?"

Griff was trying to make sense of the derelict's story. He said slowly, "Whoever *they* are, they left the buggy behind; so they can't have been figuring to take her any great distance. Does that give you any ideas?"

Malloy shook his head. "Can't say that it does."

"I'm getting one! It doesn't seem to make any kind of sense, but I've got to check it out. You with me?"

The conviction in Griff's tone made his companion answer quickly, "All the way!"

"Then come along. . . ."

Chapter Thirteen

Someone had done an expert job with the knots that held Nan Harper: Her ankles were tied to chair legs, her wrists crossed behind her and lashed to the framework of the chair. She had no idea where she was. The cloth covering her eyes took care of that, despite her every attempt to work the blindfold loose. She had finally stopped straining to free herself. Her wrists had grown swollen with the effort, and a finger of her right hand still hurt where her grandmother's ring had been unceremoniously yanked from it. Resigned, she forced herself to regain her composure as what seemed like endless hours crawled by, while she sat alone in this blind darkness.

The man who tied her had given her a rough warning: "Remember, it won't do you any good yelling for help. Nobody's gonna hear you—and even if they do, all it will get you is that I'll come back and shove a gag in your mouth. You won't like that!"

She should be grateful for having the option, she thought, and heeded the warning. Afterward, as the time passed, she listened for any sound that might tell her of her whereabouts. She heard, as from a distance, the muffled sound of talk that swelled occasionally into argument or laughter and then subsided. Once or twice she thought she heard a woman's voice. The sounds made her wonder if there was a barroom somewhere in this building where she was being held prisoner.

With no way to judge the time, except from her own cramped muscles and the gnawing of hunger, Nan couldn't tell if it was still afternoon or if evening had come. A treadmill of futile speculation, tinged by fear, to which she stubbornly refused to give way, ended suddenly, and her head lifted as she heard the metallic scrape of a key turning in a lock.

The door opened. Nan went tense as someone came toward her. Dishes and silverware on a tray made a noise as they were set down, and suddenly an odor of food sharpened the hunger pangs she had been increasingly aware of.

The same voice she'd heard earlier said gruffly, "I brought you grub. I'm gonna undo your hands so you can eat. But you be careful!"

Nan said stiffly, "Thank you. I will."

The rope was loosened and fell away. She winced as she first moved her stiff arms. Her next action was to reach up and jerk the blindfold from her eyes, blinking when light struck them.

The light was dim. Dusk showed beyond a window that had its shade pulled to the sill. Nan found she was in a small room that was almost filled by a round, green-topped table and a few straight wooden chairs. An oil lamp hung, unlighted, from the ceiling. She had never seen a private gambling room but wondered if she might be in one now. On the table, near enough for her to reach, she saw the food—a tin plate containing cooked meat, beans, a slab of bread, and eating utensils; there was also a tin cup filled with black, steaming coffee.

She wanted to bend and free her ankles, but knew she would not be allowed to try. The man who had untied her hands now moved into view, coming around in front of her to turn one of the chairs and straddle it, his arms folded on its back. She recognized him; he was one of the pair who had seized her on their second attempt—a bony, red-headed fellow with a scurf of unshaven whiskers, a sullen eye, and a gun at his belt.

As she stared at him he scowled and said, "It's a waste of time for you, tryin' to remember what I look like. You won't be seein' me again."

"Why are you doing this to me?" she demanded. "What is it getting anyone? How can I persuade you to let me go?"

The muddy eyes looked back at her without expression, showing he had no intention of answering. Without wasting more time on him, Nan turned to see what he had brought for her to eat.

The food was poor enough—the beans scorched, the roast beef undercooked, the coffee bitter. She knew there was no point in complaining, and she was going to need whatever food she could get. She deliberately went to work at it, meanwhile taking up a more careful surveillance of this room where she found herself imprisoned. But there was little enough she had missed in the first hasty glance.

All the time she was emptying her plate, her jailer sat motionless, seemingly uninterested. The moment she finished and pushed the utensils away, however, he was on his feet again. As he came toward her she wondered for a desperate moment if she dared risk trying to get a hand on that gun, but she wasn't given the chance. He seized her arms and pulled them around behind her chair, and with his superior strength held them imprisoned while he once more put the rope to them.

Nan tried surreptitiously to fight for slack, but he was too wary. None too gently he lashed her wrists to the chair's frame, as tightly as before. And having tested the knots to his satisfaction, he gathered up the tinware and turned toward the door without a further word.

It was only then she realized he had either completely forgotten the blindfold or had decided he would spare her that. She was certainly not going to raise the question; she held her tongue. The door closed behind him. The key turned in the lock, and she was once more alone.

Despite the pain in her wrists, she spent some minutes testing the new knots before deciding it would do no good. She listened for every sound while her thoughts worked uselessly at the few words she had got from her jailer, and the remaining light in the room swiftly thickened and became full night. She could no longer even make out a faint indication of where the window should be.

Complete darkness somehow made things worse. She had to fight against a growing despair and fright.

Again, all judgment as to the passing of time failed her. It might have been hours, or only a fraction of one, when a heavy tread of boots approached the door and paused there. Once more the key turned and the door opened.

Nan caught her breath as she saw, faintly silhouetted against lamplight in the hallway outside, a bulky figure that struck her as somehow familiar. The man paused only briefly on the threshold. After that he entered, heading directly for the table. Still unable to see him clearly, Nan watched with the breath shallow in her throat as he did something to the ceiling lamp. She heard the glass shade cranked upward; suddenly a match flared and he held it to the wick. The flickering light of the match fell upon his upraised face, and Nan gasped in disbelief, knowing why she had thought she recognized the shape of the man.

It was Tom Riordan—bodyguard to Morgan Slaughter.

The room seemed to spin around her while she tried to make sense of this. Was he here, perhaps, to rescue her? Riordan was scowling in concentration as he got the lamp burning and the shade settled in place. That done, he turned again to the door, with no more than a glance at her. Standing inside the room, he swung the door shut and locked it with the key he had removed and placed in his pocket when he entered.

He came back to her then—and halted in his tracks as he apparently got his first clear sight of her, watching him from the chair where she sat bound. His shock appeared every bit as great as hers. His head jerked back; his heavy features twisted, and an obscenity was jarred from him. He blurted out, "I thought I gave orders to keep you blindfolded!"

Though confused and bewildered, Nan found the self-control to retort coldly, "What is it, Mr. Riordan? You came to have a look at your prisoner—not knowing that I was going to be able to *see* you?"

Anger replaced his first stunned reaction. Heavy jaw muscles tightened as he gritted his teeth, scowling at her. But then, apparently deciding that what was done could not be undone, he gave a loose shrug. "Well." He grunted. "So you've had an eyeful. What the hell difference, I guess." He pulled a chair out, dropped into it, and leaned a heavy forearm on the table. Thick fingers drummed the green cloth as he stared silently at Nan.

Nan had always been somewhat afraid of this man, but just now, tied and helpless as she was, anger overcame her fear. "Will you tell me what this is all about?" she demanded, meeting his look. "What is it you want from me? I've nothing of any value—except for the ring somebody has already pulled off my finger. And that certainly isn't worth anything to anyone but me."

Riordan showed her a twisted grin. "You think not? We needed it—for proof. We figure it's gonna be worth fifty thousand dollars to us!"

"Proof?" she echoed, and suddenly her eyes widened in horror. "Oh, no! You sent it to Grandpa, didn't you—to show that you're really holding me prisoner! Oh, how *dare* you? He's an old man, and he isn't well. It's cruel to give him such a shock. It—it might have killed him!"

Riordan merely shrugged again, and then he took a whiskey bottle from a pocket of his coat. It was all but a quarter empty, and by the shine of his eyes Nan thought he must have downed a good part of the other three-quarters in the past few hours. He pushed out the cork with one broad thumb, and without answering her, he tilted the bottle to his mouth and took a healthy shot.

"What else did you say? You're asking fifty thousand to get me back? That's insane! Near broke as we are right now, he'd do well to raise fifty!"

"Hell!" Riordan slammed the table with one hard palm. "You think we don't know that? The old bastard has nothing at all to do with this business, once he's identified the ring."

His smug confidence infuriated her and made her reckless. "You seem awfully sure of yourself! Do you think I'm too afraid to go to the marshal after I get out of here? Or to tell your employer? In case you hadn't noticed, Morgan Slaughter has shown a lot of concern about Grandpa and me. How long do you suppose you'll keep your job, once he learns what you've been up to behind his back."

Riordan's eyes hardened. "Bitch!" In that moment Nan thought he was going to get up from his chair and strike her across the face. She braced herself for it, but instead he appeared to remember the bottle at his elbow. He snatched it up, tilted it, and drained the rest of its contents in a couple of swallows; then he tossed it on the table and wiped a wrist across his mouth.

Suddenly, in a startling change of mood, something struck him funny and his laughter rolled through the room while Nan stared at him in bewilderment and disbelief. Finally calm enough to speak, Riordan bared his teeth in a grin and exclaimed, "That's the biggest joke I ever heard! So he took you in, too, did he?"

"Who?" she demanded. "What are you talking about?"

"Why, this 'Mr. Slaughter' of yours! He's made fools of everybody. You and old Bill, and that dumb Horace Tabor—the whole town of Leadville! I bet it never entered your head that what happened to you today was his doing."

Nan was thunderstruck. "That's ridiculous. You're lying!"

"Lying, am I?" He shook his head. "You really have been taken in—like all the rest. Remember a couple of weeks back—there was that scene in the middle of Harrison Avenue? Well, Slaughter put on a real good show that day to make you think he didn't like the way I was treating that bastard Malloy."

"There's nothing you can tell me about that," Nan retorted. "Mr. Slaughter gave you a tongue-lashing, and even struck you in the face. I *saw* it!"

"You saw what you were meant to see! Afterward he apologized to me, but he didn't need to—I knew that had just been for your benefit. Me and him, we understand each other. We're practically partners!"

Riordan loomed over her, pointing his finger at her. "Let me give it to you straight! Two months ago, this gent you call Morgan Slaughter found out from a geologist he'd bribed that the Silver Star mine, next to his Horseshoe, had just run into a fault and lost all trace of the rich vein they'd been following. From the report, he knew the very same thing was gonna happen to him. That meant the only decent strike he'd managed to develop on that property was about due to pinch out and leave him broke—unless he found a sucker to unload it on. First, though, he needed to close down operations before work went any farther—and before the fault was found and the bad news had a chance to leak out. So he did it by getting the miners to go out on strike!"

Nan said scornfully, "How could anybody do that?"

"Oh, hell. Easy enough! All it takes is a few spies on the payroll, who can be trusted to spread rumors. He saw to it a story got around that the owners had all agreed to cut wages to two seventy-five a day as soon as the railroads begun shippin' in cheap labor. Didn't take much of that kind of talk to have Malloy and the rest mad enough to pull them out of the pits and shut everything tight as a drum."

Nan stared. "Are you saying Slaughter deliberately

goaded his workers into walking out? And then brought in hired toughs to use against them?"

Riordan shrugged. "He had to make it look good, didn't he? Couldn't allow any risk of terms being reached and the mines reopened, so that the world could learn the Horseshoe was worthless! That would have spoiled the whole game for him." And listening, Nan suddenly had to admit that Morgan Slaughter, under the right circumstances, might just be capable of such convoluted scheming.

But she shook her head. "I still don't understand. Even supposing it's all true—where do *I* fit in? What has all this to do with Grandpa and me?"

"You?" The man snorted contemptuously. "You actually thought, account of him playing up to you like he's been doing, that you really had him interested, didn't you? That's what he wanted everybody to think! But, hell, I can tell you, you ain't his type." Eyeing her boldly, Riordan openly sneered. "Damned if I can think whose type you *would* be. A gent wants something more on the lines of a *real* woman . . . like that Baby Doe of Tabor's, now. . . ."

Stung by his words in spite of herself, Nan felt her cheeks grow warm. But she retorted, "I don't need someone like you to tell me my shortcomings! I've always known I was plain—it's the very reason I never could understand what Morgan Slaughter found attractive in me, especially since I certainly never gave him any encouragement. It's easy enough for me to believe he was pretending—but I still don't see what use it might have been to him."

"I guess I'll have to spell it out, just to give you an idea of the way a smart man operates. Today, everything finally came to a head. On Slaughter's advice, Tabor called in the governor against the strikers. Then somebody topped that by taking a shot in Tabor's direction—that about scared the son of a bitch to death, just like it was meant to."

His tone and smug expression revealed the truth to

her. "That was *you*, wasn't it? *You* fired that rifle—simply to frighten him. All part of the plan!"

Riordan didn't bother denying it. He picked up the bottle, but then remembered with a grunt that it was empty. Tossing it aside, he got up and went to the door. He unlocked it and poked his head outside. She heard him give an order to someone in the hallway: "Hey, MacIvor! Fetch me another bottle from the bar." The brief burst of noise that had come with the door's opening ended as he shut it again and turned the key in the lock.

He seemed to have another of his abrupt changes of mood. As though grown tired of this scene, instead of seating himself again he came and stood over her, arms akimbo, while he finished his story in short order. "So now you're being held, for the ransom price of giving in to every demand the strikers have been making—and in addition, fifty thousand dollars in cash. Everybody knows just who *that's* aimed at. Slaughter has promised to pay the ransom himself, even if it means sacrificing the Horseshoe. Understand? He's offered it to Horace Tabor for fifty thousand, if Tabor will just raise the cash to set you free. And Tabor's getting that together for him, right now."

"And what happens when Horace Tabor finds out he's been taken in? That Slaughter had me kidnapped, and the mine he's bought is really worthless?"

Riordan laughed loosely. "Once Slaughter has his hands on the money—tonight—me and him are leaving this place. So it won't matter what Tabor finds out, or what you tell him. There won't be a damn thing he can do about it! I just wish I could see the look on his face when the bastard learns how he got took—to the tune of fifty grand!" His grin spread as he saw the final, shocked understanding in her face. Abruptly, then, he turned away to the sound of a knock at the door.

A voice outside said, "I brought your bottle." But when Riordan turned the key and flung the door open, it was not MacIvor he faced but Griff Cameron. And instead of a whiskey bottle, what Griff had in his hand was a revolver.

For a long moment the men faced each other in the doorway, before Riordan recovered from his surprise and moved to slam the door shut again.

Griff was quicker, catching the door on one shoulder and pushing on through; Riordan, off balance, was driven back. He staggered against the edge of the green-topped table and braced himself there as he pawed for his gun. He got it out of the holster and then somehow lost it when Griff's weight struck and jarred it loose from his hand.

"Don't move!" Griff raised his own weapon, threatening. I'll use this if I have to!"

In his hatred of Griff Cameron, Riordan refused to yield. His mouth twisted and a bent knee came up, trying for his enemy's groin. Quickly twisting his body, Griff thwarted that move, but Riordan retaliated by driving a fist at Griff's head. Griff was driven, reeling, against the wall, which shook with the impact of his weight. There was a sharp outcry from Nan, as she saw Griff slide down the rough wall and land, prone, at the base of it.

Riordan looked around, hastily searching for the gun he had lost. He never reached it. Griff was still conscious, and he steadied his wrist against the floor and fired a shot into the ceiling, above Riordan's head.

The report was thunderous in that enclosed space. Riordan, jerking about, saw the smoking gun muzzle aimed squarely at him. It was enough to make him forget his own weapon. For a tense moment the two men's eyes met. Then, driven by desperation, Riordan turned and hurled himself through the open doorway, risking another bullet—which never came.

The corridor, which split the rear of this long, one-story structure housing Drago's gambling hall, was dimly lighted by a single oil lamp in a wall holder. A rear door offered escape to the night outside. But instead of using it Riordan turned in the other direction, toward the bar, where he knew he would find help from some of the toughs he'd hired, with the mineowners' money, for use against the striking miners. But after one stride he abruptly halted.

Mike Malloy stood facing him, with the light of a wall lamp gleaming on the revolver in his work-roughened hand. Lying in a sprawl in front of him was MacIvor—the man Riordan had sent to fetch the whiskey, but who seemed to have been knocked out by a blow from a gun barrel instead. Malloy's gun was pointed squarely at Riordan, and the Irishman said, "Were you headin' somewhere? I think you'll be turnin' around and steppin' ahead of me, back into that room instead!"

Riordan's empty hands clenched in frustration and rage. "Get out of my way!" he said harshly. "I'll break you in two!"

In answer, Malloy pulled back the hammer; the clicks of the revolver going into full cock were distinct and threatening there in the dead stillness of the hallway. Weaponless, Riordan was painfully aware that at any moment Griff Cameron might be coming out of the room, bringing a second revolver against him.

But then came other sounds, from beyond Malloy— the swelling of voices and the pounding of boots from the barroom at the front of the gambling hall. Riordan saw alarm sweep across the Irishman's face. The patrons of Drago's, hearing a gunshot, were on their way to investigate. Malloy hastily swung around and put his shoulders against the wall. Even though his gun was still trained on his prisoner, the approaching danger clearly distracted him . . . and Tom Riordan saw his chance.

He took one cautious step back, then another. In a single burst of movement, he whirled and made the distance to the door to the alley, wrenched it open, and dived through.

He thoroughly expected a bullet to follow him, but his sudden dash to escape must have taken Malloy by surprise. The door slammed shut, and Riordan was alone

in the dark alley, the night air chill against his face, which
had gone wet with sweat. He mopped it with a sleeve.

The last few minutes had knocked all the effects of
the liquor out of him, and suddenly he felt completely
sober—and alarmed, too, as he thought of the drunken
bragging he had done in front of that damned Harper
woman! But an instant later he forgot that, as the sound of
many guns going off spilled from the hallway he had just
left. As he heard the shots, Riordan's upper lip pulled
back, showing his yellowed teeth in a fierce grin.

Hell, he had nothing at all to worry about! Griff and
Malloy were as good as dead, against odds like those. The
boys could take care of them; right now it was almost time
for him to join his partner and collect the money from
Horace Tabor. Once they had that fifty grand, there was
no way this town would hold them. The final payoff for
weeks of careful scheming was nearly at hand. . . .

Chapter Fourteen

Griff Cameron was already working at the knots that held Nan Harper prisoner when Mike Malloy came bursting into the card room and hurriedly slammed the door after him. Griff demanded, "What became of Riordan?"

The Irishman grimaced. "I had him but he got away—slipped out the alley door when them others came at me." The sounds of yelling men echoed through the narrow hallway. Malloy gave the key a turn in the lock and added bleakly, "*That* ain't going to stop 'em for long."

"The table . . ." Griff said.

He gave it a shove toward the door, and together they toppled the heavy piece of furniture there for a barricade. The next moment, when someone's weight struck the door, it held, and Malloy fired a shot, aiming above the heads of the men outside. A startled yelp and a scramble of boots mingled with the sound of the gunshot; an answering bullet drilled the door, leaving a round black hole in the wood. Malloy ducked behind the tabletop, swearing.

Griff ordered sharply, "Keep them busy!" and went back to the task of releasing the frightened woman.

More than one of the men crowded in the hall opened fire. Malloy, crouched behind the table, fired back blindly and brought a yelp from someone on the other side of the partition. The firing ceased, for the moment anyhow. Griff, impatient with the knots, remembered he had a knife in his pocket. He whipped it out, thumbed open a blade, and went to work with that.

"How did you ever find me?" Nan asked in a trembling voice.

"Wasn't too hard." In a few terse words he explained about finding her abandoned rig a few doors up the street. "We figured they couldn't have taken you far. Then I remembered this place—a hangout for the enemies of the strikers. And since *somebody* was trying to put the blame for this on Malloy and his friends, it seemed worth checking out." When the last knot fell away, he helped her up, his grip tight on her arm as her stiffened limbs made her momentarily unsteady. "Are you all right?" he asked.

"Yes. Oh, but Griff! I have so much to tell you!"

"It'll have to wait." He turned to the room's single window, flung up the shade, found the catch that locked the window, and hastily lifted the sash. The dark narrow walkway between Drago's and an adjoining building was outside. Griff slid a leg through and then, his gun ready, let himself down into weeds below the window. All seemed well; he called to Nan and helped her to follow him. Moments later, after one final shot through the bullet-riddled door he had been guarding, Mike Malloy joined them. Griff caught Nan's hand and moved away at a run, with Malloy as rear guard.

State Street was tuning up its raucous voice for the night, demonstrating its claim to being the toughest section of Leadville. But no one interfered with the three fugitives from Drago's, and they were surprised to find that Nan's rig still stood where it had been left. As Griff handed Nan up to the seat and went around to take his place beside her, Malloy overtook them. "Nobody seems to be following us yet," he reported.

Griff nodded. "Good! Climb in—we'll take Nan home."

But she caught at his sleeve, urgently. "You *must* listen to me! Tom Riordan was drunk and bragging. You'll never believe the things he told me!"

"What kind of things?" Griff demanded, and listened in growing astonishment as she poured out her story.

Malloy, crowded on the seat with them, swore softly when she had finished. "Tom Riordan never had brains enough to make up a brag like that!" he said, looking across Nan at Griff. "What he said is all true, ain't it?"

Griff nodded bleakly. "Oh, yes. It's all true!"

"But there's more!" Nan insisted, breaking in on them. Griff sensed her reluctance as she braced herself to continue. "A man came into the office this afternoon. He called himself Vern Showalt—said he was looking for someone named Connors. He—he showed me a picture. . . ."

It was like a dash of cold water. Griff stiffened, knowing now that it had *not* been imagination that disturbed him earlier, but the reality of the man himself—the pursuer who had finally trailed him here. Griff said slowly, "Did this Showalt tell you who he was? And what he wanted with the man named Connors?"

"He told me," Nan answered in a small voice. "None of it made any sense to me, and I said so! I just couldn't believe there was a word of truth in it."

Griff drew a breath. "Sometimes appearances can be dead set against someone," he said slowly. "But appearances can be wrong."

"Oh, I know!"

Their eyes met in the shadows of the buggy top. Griff found her hand and gave it a squeeze, to show his gratitude. Her hand felt cold, and it trembled.

"But that man Showalt was in deadly earnest!" Nan insisted. "If—if I were Connors, I'd get out of Leadville—at once! I wouldn't stop for anything—just get a horse and go. . . ."

Mike Malloy was looking from one to the other, clearly

puzzled and unable to make sense of what they were saying. Keeping his own counsel, Griff slapped the reins against the rump of the bay and got the rig moving. They turned off State onto Harrison Avenue, and just ahead loomed the bulk of the Clarendon and beyond that the Opera House. Its doors stood open on the brightly lit lobby, and an audience was gathering for the evening's performance. On the second floor, more lights showed in the windows of Tabor's private office.

Without a word, Griff pulled over as near the entrance as he was able and brought the rig to a stop. Nan turned to him in consternation. "What in the world are you doing?"

"You haven't forgotten?" he said. "Slaughter is due to pick up the ransom money he tricked Horace Tabor into raising for him. Far as I'm concerned, Tabor can look out for himself—but I'd hate to think Slaughter could get away with his schemes, especially the wrong he's done to people I've come to look on as my friends."

Malloy observed, "Seems only fair Tabor should have a warning. Whether he'd believe anything *we* tried to tell him is another matter."

"He'd believe me," Nan said quietly. "By the time I got through telling what happened to me this evening— everything I saw and heard . . ."

Griff moved to step out onto the sidewalk. "Then let's go up there and see that he gets an earful."

But Nan caught at his arm. "Are you sure this is wise? After—after what I just told you?" But when she saw the look on his face, she must have decided he had made up his mind. She let him help her down, and Malloy joined them.

Because of the traffic, they had had to leave the buggy almost half a block beyond the entrance to the Opera House. As they turned in at the brightly lighted doorway, a few latecomers were still climbing the broad steps from the lobby. The auditorium doors had already been closed, and a hum of anticipation came from there, mingled with the strains of the pit orchestra tuning up. They went on past, up the next set of stairs to a corridor, where Griff had a brief glimpse, through the balcony doorway, of the noisy audience settling into place and of a fifteen-piece orchestra starting an overture. Gas footlights illuminated a curtain depicting an ancient castle rising beside a stream.

Across the hall, at the door of Tabor's suite, Nan knocked, and then knocked again.

A moment passed. Then the door was opened by Baby Doe, who stared at them with a look of disbelief on her beautiful features. Beyond her, Griff saw Horace Tabor seated behind a massive desk; and there was old Bill Harper, clutching the arms of his chair, his mouth fallen open in astonishment.

Baby Doe found the voice to cry out, "Nan! Come in—come in! My God, we've been so worried about you! Tell me, what in the world—?"

When Nan answered, there was a tremor in her voice that Griff knew must be from exhaustion, after her ordeal. She passed a hand across her forehead and said, "Not now. There's something I have to say to Mr. Tabor. And it won't wait!"

Horace Tabor seemed to age in the few minutes it took for him to hear Nan's story. He settled deeper into his padded desk chair, his head fallen forward. When she finished, there was a long silence, during which a roar of laughter and applause swept the auditorium and reached faintly to the people in this quiet office. Finally Tabor straightened his shoulders. He passed a palm across his luxuriant mustache and said, in a heavy tone, "I never liked bein' lied to!"

Nan protested quickly, "Mr. Tabor, I swear that every word I've told you—"

He flapped a hand at her, shaking his balding head. "I don't mean you, Nan. I've known both you and your grandfather too long to doubt you, for a minute. . . ." He sighed deeply. "Just the same, it gravels a man to have to admit he's been made a fool of!"

Griff could hear the bitterness in his voice. He guessed that Tabor was a man who felt pride in his accomplishments and was sensitive to those who claimed that his success was all a matter of blind luck and had nothing to do with his own intelligence. Now Tabor looked at Malloy, who stood in the background without offering any comment. "Tell me somethin', Malloy," he said, "and I want the truth! Have you, or any of your people, been makin' threats about puttin' a torch to this building?"

Malloy stared. "Burn the Opera House?" he echoed, aghast. "By all the saints in heaven—no! Why, *you* couldn't be no prouder of this theater than we are, Mr. Tabor, for what it means to Leadville. I just wish, once in a while, I could afford the price of tickets for myself and my Mary— and they wouldn't have to be box seats, either. The balcony would do fine. But as for burning it down, if anybody says he heard such talk from *us*, then he's lyin' in his teeth!"

Nobody could have doubted his sincerity. Griff saw it hit Tabor, saw him scowl over it like a man facing a painful reassessment of his thoughts. "I've been lied to, all right!" Tabor straightened in his chair, and when he lifted his head, it was with a new air of resolution. "Malloy," he said, "you've got yourself a box waitin' in the Opera House for whenever you want to use it. Now, can you get some of your people together and bring them here, say, ten o'clock tomorrow mornin', so we can sit down and talk over this strike situation? Maybe it would do some good."

Malloy looked like a man unable to believe his ears, but he quickly recovered. "If you really think it could," he agreed, "of course I'll pass the word."

Tabor nodded. "Good!" He added, "There's one more thing you can do for me if you will. I need Marshal Osland here, in case Slaughter has the nerve to try to collect this

money for the worthless mine he almost unloaded on me."
He indicated a tin box that lay on the desk in front of him.
"Will you go see if you can find the marshal and say I sent
for him?"

A broad grin split the Irishman's face. "Sure, an' it'd
be a pleasure, Mr. Tabor!" he exclaimed.

"And tell him to hurry! Slaughter is overdue now."

"I'm on my way!" A moment later, Malloy was gone.

As the door closed behind him, cutting off another
brief burst of sound from the show in progress, Bill Harper
drew a breath and said, "My! It's been quite an evening!
But we've got Nan back, safe and sound. I guess there's no
more reason for us to be taking up your time, Horace."
He put heavily veined hands on the arms of his chair and
looked around for someone to make the first move toward
departing.

"Well . . ." Tabor frowned, hesitating. "Bill, it's up to
you and your granddaughter, of course, but I'd be grateful
if you both would stay. I'd like to hear her repeat what
she's been tellin' me in front of Slaughter and the marshal.
Fastest way I know to lay it all on the table and get to the
bottom of this thing."

Baby Doe, who had been standing at the window,
turned in quick protest. "That isn't fair, Horace!" she
exclaimed. "After all Nan's been through, you've got no
right to ask that."

He frowned, but accepted the rebuke. "I suppose
not. Forget I suggested it."

"No, it's all right!" Nan Harper said. "I don't mind.
After all, Marshal Osland will be wanting to hear my
story, sooner or later. We might as well get it over
with."

Silent during all this, Griff had stood behind Nan's
chair with arms folded, leaning his shoulders against the
wall. He straightened now as he said sharply, "I don't like
this! Like Mrs. Doe said, Nan's been through more than
enough without making her confront Morgan Slaughter.

She shouldn't be put through that right now. How do you know what he might take it into his head to do?"

"I said the idea didn't bother me," Nan insisted. "Grandpa can wait here with me. But I happen to know," she told Tabor, "there's something else Mr. Cameron should be doing just now, and *he* won't be able to stay. Isn't that right, Griff?" And though she spoke matter-of-factly, the look she gave him was one almost of pleading— begging for him to go.

He met the look, reading her anxiety, knowing her concern for him and for the danger he was putting himself in during every moment he spent here, with Vern Showalt so close upon his heels.

Tabor's attention had been drawn to him now, and he eyed the stranger as he pawed at his flowing mustache. "Cameron . . . I guess we ain't exactly met. If we have you to thank for comin' to Nan's rescue and bringin' her back to us, then I calculate we're all indebted to you."

"Don't let it bother you." Griff turned and picked up his hat from the table where he had laid it. "What she says is true; I have to be leaving—tonight. I don't reckon I'll be coming back to Leadville." But then a thought made him pause, his eyes narrowing. He indicated the box on the desk in front of Tabor. "It's none of my business, of course—but if you've got cash there, I'd suggest you get it out of sight before Morgan Slaughter shows up. The man's gone to a lot of trouble and conniving to get that money from you. Why tempt him?"

Tabor nodded his agreement. "Makes sense," he said shortly. "I'll just stick it in the safe."

He rose, taking the money, and started toward a large steel box that stood in a corner of the room. Griff found himself facing Bill Harper, who was on his feet now, his weathered face gone suddenly pale with distress.

Harper put out a hand, as though to clutch at Griff's coat. He let the hand drop as he cried, "You ain't really going? Here I've kept hoping all along you'd change your mind and throw in with me and Nan. I don't see how I can make it any plainer, how bad you're needed!"

His voice was trembling as he finished. Griff was touched with something more than pity. He was quite sincere as he told the old man, "I'm truly sorry—believe me, I'd like to stay. I've been thinking there could maybe be a way, with a loan from Tabor or someone, to pack up that operation of yours and move it south to Arizona or someplace, where there's room for another stage line." He shook his head. "But—something's come up. I haven't any choice."

Nan put in, "He just can't, Grandpa—honestly. He's explained the whole situation to me." And hearing that, the old man accepted it without any more argument, even though disappointment bowed his head and he seemed to shrink in on himself a little. Griff, before he turned away, paused to let his hand rest for a moment on Nan's shoulder. Their eyes met, and he knew that she read the meaning he tried to put into his touch—a message of farewell, one that had to be given wordlessly.

Glancing past her then, he saw Baby Doe watching them. There was something in her expression that told him this woman, who for all her blond beauty he had thought of as shallow and completely self-centered, seemed to have at least some inkling of what passed between him and Nan. Her eyes were full of sympathy.

He gave Nan a last look and attempted a smile that held all his feelings. Then he forced himself to turn his back on that room and let himself into the corridor.

Griff left in a turmoil of emotions; sounds of laughter and applause from the auditorium made an ironic contrast, seeming to pursue him as he made his way down the stairs and out of the theater. The thought of all he was leaving was even worse than knowing that from now on he would be a man on the dodge, with a bloodhound named Vern Showalt on his tail and no real hope of clearing himself.

In addition, Nan's determination to stay and confront Morgan Slaughter worried him. Seeing his schemes collapse, Slaughter would be a desperate man, capable of doing almost anything. Even the marshal—supposing he got to Tabor's office in time—might not be able to prevent an explosion.

It was all he could do to keep from turning back. But the parting had been cruel enough for them all, unbearable to repeat; since Nan had found the courage to help him leave, he had to go through with it.

His face was bleak as he dropped down the wide flight of steps into the empty lobby. The ticket office had been closed, but the doors to the street stood open. Just as Griff reached them, he saw a pair of horsemen dismounting in front of the brightly lit building. One look and he took a hurried, sideward step that placed him against one of the folded-back leaves of the door, out of sight. He pushed his coat aside and put his hand on the Smith and Wesson.

Morgan Slaughter had put his horse into the narrow gap between a couple of parked carriages. As he stepped onto the boardwalk fronting the Opera House, Tom Riordan was close at his heels. Riordan tried to catch his boss's arm, protesting something, but Slaughter shook him off. Looking past the edge of the door, Griff saw the ugly look on the mineowner's face and heard clearly his terse and angry speech.

"I've had all I can take out of you in one night!" Slaughter said, voice dripping with scorn. "You get drunk, after I warn you to stay sober. You blab everything you know in front of that bitch—and later we find out that she flew the coop and got clean away from Drago's. Haven't you done enough?"

Riordan turned sullen but was stubborn. "All right!" he shot back. "So I made a mistake. But we'll do worse if we walk into a trap!"

"You don't expect me to leave this town empty-handed!" the other man retorted. "The game's not over yet, in spite of what you did. There's fifty grand waiting up there in Tabor's office—and nothing can keep me from getting it. I don't care who tries to stop me or who I have to kill!"

He brushed past the big Irishman and started again, purposefully, toward the wide doorway. Riordan shook his heavy head with a groan. "Wait!" he cried in desperation. And then came the words that caused the small hairs to lift on Griff's neck. *"For God's sake, Milo—"*

Almost without thinking, Griff came around the edge of the door and into the open. At sight of him, with his hand clamped on the butt of a holstered revolver, the pair halted. In the glare of the street lamps, with the lobby at Griff's back, the three of them stood motionless as Griff said, "So it's Milo, is it? I might have guessed! It was *you* that killed Lew Burke during that holdup—while Riordan kept his gun on the passengers, and Ed Luft held me back from interfering!"

If he expected a denial, they surprised him. Without any change of expression, the man who now called himself Morgan Slaughter answered bluntly, "I've been wondering when you were going to catch on. You handed me kind of a jolt the other day, when I saw you get off the stage—until it became clear Luft was the only one you were on to."

Griff nodded. "So when Luft laid for me in my hotel room, he was all primed with a story about his partners being long gone, so I wouldn't have any reason to keep hunting for them. It never occurred to me that he was lying. Who'd have thought a big mineowner, here in Leadville, would have had any part in holding up a stage in Montana?" He made a sudden shrewd guess. "Or did it have something to do with your mine going busted, like Riordan told Nan this evening?"

"I was caught short of cash, as a matter of fact," the other man answered readily enough. "The three of us used to work as a team, in the old days before I turned respectable and took a new name. It came in very handy that Luft should have got word to us, just when he did, about his deal with that stage guard to tip him off when the bank shipment was due. So Tom and I took us a week off to ride up to Montana and help knock it over."

"And murder Lew Burke, as soon as you were through with him!"

Slaughter shrugged. "Only one good way to make sure a man keeps his mouth shut."

In a voice like flint, Riordan added, "Including *yours*, you bastard!"

Warned by his tone of what was coming, Griff was already pulling at his revolver. He cleared his holster at almost the same instant as Riordan. Both weapons exploded, almost together, but Riordan's bullet went harmlessly into the boards under Griff's feet. Riordan wasn't so lucky, and he stumbled back against the wheel of a parked carriage and bounced off it, going first to his knees and then dropping full length, mortally wounded.

All too aware of Morgan Slaughter—or Milo, or whatever his true name was—Griff tried now to locate his other enemy. In doing so, he pivoted on the low stone step and met disaster. His boot slipped off the step, and he lost his balance and found himself going down, in an odd kind of slow motion. He put out both hands to catch himself, and the hard edge of the step gave his forearm a numbing blow as he landed on it. In a helpless reflex his fingers opened, and the Smith and Wesson jumped out of his fist.

Sprawled there, he looked for Slaughter and saw the man pacing toward him, not hurrying, a look of cruel satisfaction etched into his features. Slaughter's gun was in his hand and pointed at Griff's head. Deliberately, he struck Griff's fallen weapon with the edge of his foot and sent it skittering farther out of reach. He took careful aim as he said distinctly, "Good-bye—damn you!"

The gunshot Griff was braced for came from some-where above and behind him. Uncomprehendingly, he saw Slaughter blown aside by the impact of lead, to hit the sidewalk rolling and then lie suddenly and completely limp. Stunned, Griff twisted then and peered up through acrid powder smoke at Vern Showalt, looming over him.

The express company detective looked back, holding the gun with which he had shot Morgan Slaughter. "Are you hurt?" he demanded.

Griff shook his head. "No."

"You're a lucky man. . . ."

Griff tried to absorb this, even to understand how this man could be here. He managed to ask, "Did you hear any of what we said?"

"I heard enough," Showalt answered. "Like I told you—you're a lucky man, Griff Connors!"

He left him and went to have a look at the sprawled figures of Slaughter and Riordan, both lifeless. Coming upon the revolver Griff had lost, he picked it up and without a word handed it to its owner. That simple ges-ture told Griff, as nothing else could, that Vern Showalt was satisfied with what he had heard and seen, and that the charge against him was cleared.

Griff holstered the gun as he got to his feet, suddenly aware of the activity around him. Moments before, with the fading of the gunshots, this section of street had lain nearly silent except for the startled horses snorting and fidgeting. Now, almost from nowhere, a crowd had gath-ered, and the night was split by excited voices. Above his head a window of Horace Tabor's office had been opened; it looked like Tabor himself leaning there, trying to see what was happening.

Then as Griff turned back into the lobby, he heard a sound of light and hurrying footsteps, and suddenly Nan Harper appeared, rushing pell-mell down the steps. She passed the closed doors of the auditorium, where the performance continued, undisturbed by the gunfire outside. She was halfway down the lobby staircase before she caught sight of Griff and halted—one hand at her throat, the other gripping the rail as though to steady her. Her eyes were wide and her face had gone pale with emotion. To Griff she had never appeared more attractive than in that moment.

Nan was still poised there, motionless and trembling in relief at seeing him whole and unharmed, when Griff climbed the last remaining steps and took her in his arms.

Author's Note

Leadville's 1880 strike was not its last. Sixteen years later, the miners again went out, but this time the strike was prolonged, destructive, and led to loss of life. Troops were called in, and the strike was crushed; the miners had to surrender without any gain after eight months of sacrifice.

Most of the fabulous mines that made Leadville a legend have long since been closed. Some of the landmarks of the old town—notably, the Tabor Opera House—still stand, but many more, including the Clarendon Hotel, have vanished. Today, the old town lives largely on its memories.

As for Horace Tabor, he got a divorce from Augusta—at the price of a settlement that made her a wealthy woman for the rest of her days. He married Baby Doe on March 1, 1883, in a lavish ceremony held at Willard's Hotel in Washington, D.C., where Tabor had used his money and his political influence to acquire a thirty-day appointment to the U.S. Senate. The wedding was attended by President Chester A. Arthur and by congressmen and members of the Cabinet—but *not* by their wives, who were scandalized over Tabor's divorce and remarriage.

Back again in Denver, Tabor continued to pour out his wealth in a building program—including a business

block and another, truly luxurious opera house, the Tabor
Grand—and in ever more speculative investments. But in
1893 Congress repealed the Sherman Silver-Purchase Act,
which had held the price of that metal at unrealistic levels,
and with that the bubble burst. Horace Tabor's pyramid of
wealth collapsed, and he lost everything. For a time he
was reduced to wheelbarrow work as a slagman at a
Leadville smelter—ironically, earning the same wage of
three dollars a day he had once insisted was sufficient for a
common laborer. Finally his political friends got him the
postmaster's job at Denver, which he held until his death
in April 1899.

Through the collapse of his fortune, Baby Doe stood
by her husband faithfully. Dying, he had little to leave her
aside from the deed to the once-fabulous Matchless mine
and a promise that, if she only held on to it, it would one
day make her wealthy again. So Baby Doe returned to
Leadville, where she moved into a toolshed on the Matchless and spent the rest of her life in abject poverty, dressed
in rags, trying vainly to raise funds and bring the played-
out old mine back into operation. In March 1935, when
she was eighty years old, Baby Doe was found there in her
shack, frozen to death.

STAGECOACH STATION 21:

FARGO
by Hank Mitchum

In November 1876, the Sioux are celebrating their victory at Little Big Horn five months earlier by tearing up railroad tracks throughout Montana and Dakota territories. To keep commerce and the mail moving, Chance Dayton has taken on the assignment of establishing a stagecoach run between Fort Keogh in Montana and Fargo in Dakota Territory. While setting up that route, he becomes the lone survivor of an attack by the Sioux on a cavalry troop, in which he saves the life of an Indian named North Wind.

The inaugural stage run is delayed when notorious gunslinger Dakota Smith kills one of the passengers and takes a young boy hostage. Dayton manages to rescue the boy, while Fort Keogh's marshal, Logan Banner, continues in pursuit of the killer.

The Sioux are determined that the stage will not complete its inaugural run, and Dayton's skills are put to the test when he and his passengers come under repeated attack. He gets much support from the beautiful Polly Temple and from an unexpected source—the Indian North Wind, who sacrifices his own life to protect Dayton.

Arriving in Fargo, Chance Dayton and Polly Temple discover their true feelings for each other, while Logan Banner is forced to face the truth of the identity of Dakota Smith when they come face to face in a final, bloody confrontation.

Read FARGO, on sale December 1985 wherever Bantam paperbacks are sold.